UNDER HER SKIN

MICHELLE LOVE

HOT AND STEAMY ROMANCE

CONTENTS

About the Author   vii
Sign Up to Receive Free Books   ix
Blurb   xi

1. Chapter One   1
2. Chapter Two   8
3. Chapter Three   14
4. Chapter Four   19
5. Chapter Five   25
6. Chapter Six   33
7. Chapter Seven   42
8. Chapter Eight   48
9. Chapter Nine   54
10. Chapter Ten   60
11. Chapter Eleven   66
12. Chapter Twelve   71
13. Chapter Thirteen   76
14. Chapter Fourteen   82
15. Chapter Fifteen   87
16. Chapter Sixteen   92
17. Chapter Seventeen   99
18. Chapter Eighteen   106
19. Chapter Nineteen   113
20. Chapter Twenty   122
21. Chapter Twenty-One   126
22. Chapter Twenty-Two   136
23. Chapter Twenty-Three   140
24. Chapter Twenty-Four   148
25. Chapter Twenty-Five   154
26. Chapter Twenty-Six   165
27. Chapter Twenty-Seven   171

Sign Up to Receive Free Books   175
Preview of Dr. Orgasm   177

Chapter 1	179
Chapter 2	184
Chapter 3	189
Other Books By This Author	197
About the Author	199

Made in "The United States" by:

Michelle Love

© Copyright 2020 – Michelle Love

ISBN: 978-1-64808-129-3

ALL RIGHTS RESERVED. No part of this publication may be reproduced or transmitted in any form whatsoever, electronic, or mechanical, including photocopying, recording, or by any informational storage or retrieval system without express written, dated and signed permission from the author

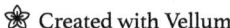 Created with Vellum

ABOUT THE AUTHOR

Mrs. Love writes about smart, sexy women and the hot alpha billionaires who love them. She has found her own happily ever after with her dream husband and adorable 6 and 2 year old kids.

Currently, Michelle is hard at work on the next book in the series, and trying to stay off the Internet.

"Thank you for supporting an indie author. Anything you can do, whether it be writing a review, or even simply telling a fellow reader that you enjoyed this. Thanks

 facebook.com/HotAndSteamyRomance
 instagram.com/michellesromance

SIGN UP TO RECEIVE FREE BOOKS

Sign Up to Receive Free E-Books and Audiobook Codes.

Would you like to read **The Unexpected Nanny, Dirty Little Virgin** and **other romance books** for **free**?

You can sign up to receive these free e-books and audiobooks by typing this link into your browser:

https://www.steamyromance.info/free-books-and-audiobooks-hot-and-steamy/

Or this one:

https://www.steamyromance.info/the-unexpected-nanny-free/

BLURB

Arrogant Italian billionaire, Arturo Bachi, is outraged when the final apartment in the building he plans to turn into a hotel is bought at an exclusive auction by someone who outbids him at the last minute. His ire fades after he meets a gorgeous young woman with whom he spends a passionate, life-altering one-night stand. Arturo is immediately enchanted; it doesn't hurt that she's the most beautiful woman he has ever seen, even if she won't tell him her real name. Though still scarred by the murder of his teenage sweetheart Flavia twenty years earlier, Arturo's frozen heart begins to thaw.

What he doesn't know is that Hero Donati is the person who bought the apartment, and she is trying to escape a terrible tragedy in her past that keeps her terrified of ever giving her heart away again. Though the two quickly begin fall in love their problems are far from over. Hero's other neighbor, George Galiano, Arturo's friend-turned-sworn-enemy makes a play for Hero's heart. Soon, Hero is trapped in a bitter war between the two men and finds herself not knowing who to trust.

Worse still, Flavia's killer makes it known that he now has Hero in his sights...

Can Arturo and Hero fight for their love, and their lives, or will they be torn apart in the most brutal and devastating way?

CHAPTER ONE

Arturo Bachi smiled at his guests as he raised his glass. "Tomorrow the final apartment in the *Villa Patrizzi* will go up for auction, and I've been assured by the seller that it will finally be mine. So, friends and fellow investors, let's drink to Lake Como's finest and most exclusive hotel—the future *Hotel Bachi!*"

His friends cheered and applauded him, and Arturo stepped off the stage to talk with his guests. After an hour where it seemed he'd shaken hands with everyone in Northern Italy, he was relieved when his best friend, Peter, spirited him away.

"Fortitude and strength," Peter grinned at his friend as they sat down at the edge of Arturo's estate, overlooking Lake Como's gentle waves. Further across the water, an alpine town nestled into the mountains softly lit up the night.

Peter had snagged a bottle of Scotch for them, and they lit cigars. Peter smiled at his friend's satisfied expression. "So close, now, Turo. Can you see it coming together quickly after the sale is settled?"

Arturo nodded. "I can. Everything is in place: the construction teams, architects. Everyone is just waiting for my go-order.

God, Peter, it seems like finally, my dream is coming true." His green eyes shone with excitement. "I was rethinking the name though. Hotel Bachi seems...a little self-indulgent."

Peter shrugged. "Not necessarily, but I take your point. The main thing is—we're close. Do you think the apartment will sell for much?"

Arturo shook his head. "It's tiny; only four rooms. I'm going to turn it into a suite with the adjoining apartment. I think I'll get it for a steal; the Board has set a price limit, so after we secure it, we'll be able to afford to go ahead with every design feature as planned."

He sighed as he continued, "A part of me wishes that I'd used my own money, then I wouldn't have to answer to anyone about budgets. But my accountant wouldn't let me." He shot a mock-scowl over to his friend, who shrugged good-naturedly.

"I just didn't want you to go broke, buddy. With this and your other hotels around the world...you're stretching yourself, and you know it. You can't rely on your trust fund to keep you afloat. Philipo could withdraw it at any moment."

Arturo sighed. His uncle Philipo had been made executor of Arturo's father's will because Arturo was too young to take over the company after Frederico died. Soon after, the grieving teenager had tumbled into alcohol and drugs, and since then, Philipo had handed out Arturo's inheritance in regulated increments. Arturo would inherit the bulk of his inheritance—nearly a billion Euros—at age forty. He both admired and resented his uncle for his decisions, but his caution had forced Arturo to leave the wild life behind and work towards his own fortune. Property had been Arturo's chosen career path and, with his natural talent and flair for it, he had earned his first billion Euros by the time he was thirty.

Now at thirty-nine, he was on the cusp of adding this inheritance to his own fortune and becoming one of the world's richest men. Arturo lived for his work, but he also enjoyed the trappings of his wealth, and it didn't hurt that he was considered one of Italy's—perhaps even one of the world's—handsomest and most eligible bachelors.

A face that could look warm and friendly one moment, and dangerous and brooding the next, his teenage beauty had matured into a more masculine and sculptured face: his large green eyes ringed with thick, midnight-black lashes; his brows dark and heavy; his beard trimmed but not overly fussy; his sensual mouth just a hint too full; his wild black curls untamed. It had to be said—Arturo Bachi was sensational, and he knew it.

He had no time for relationships and was always honest with his many conquests, but Arturo never slept with the same woman twice. Not since Flavia, his sweetheart in college. He had loved Flavia with all his heart: she was his future, his true north, his love. And Flavia had loved him for himself, not the rich, handsome boy born into wealth and opportunity, but the goofy, fun-loving boy with the big heart and poetry in his soul.

They were inseparable until that one fateful night when Arturo had been ten minutes late to the party, and Flavia had been taken by another man, one with hate in his heart and murder in his soul.

They had found Flavia a week later, stabbed multiple times, her body dumped in the lake. Arturo had run to the lake as soon as the news hit the radio; he had made it just in time to see her brought up onto the bank, her long, dark hair wrapped around her body, her usually dark olive skin so grey and wan. The water had washed the blood away, but Arturo could clearly see the stab wounds in her stomach—vicious, brutal. He had fallen to his knees and screamed until his friends Peter and George had come to get him.

Arturo thought of Flavia now, her kind, brown eyes shining up at him. As usual, her image turned his mind to imagining how scared, how terrified she must have been as her killer took her life.

God. An involuntary groan slipped out, and Peter glanced at his friend. "You okay?"

Arturo nodded, not trusting himself to speak. Peter, who had always been able to read Arturo's mind, looked at him with sympathy. "Flavia?"

Arturo nodded. "Maybe...*Hotel Flavia*?"

Peter sighed. "Arturo, as sweet as that gesture would be, it's not going to help you allow her to rest in peace. It's been twenty years, buddy."

Arturo nodded, knowing Peter was right. His eyes slid across the lake to George's villa. George Galliano, his other friend on that night. A friend no more.

"Hey." Peter nudged his shoulder. "Stop wallowing. Let's get back to your guests."

Arturo threw back the rest of his Scotch, his gaze returning to the almost empty villa across the lake: *Villa Patrizzi* that he owned 99 percent of right now. Tomorrow, it would belong to him entirely.

He couldn't wait.

HERO DONATI LOOKED around the tiny apartment. She had persuaded the realtor to let her in, even this late at night, so she could be prepared for tomorrow. This place was perfect: tiny, compact, but with a balcony that looked out over the lake where she could sit and sketch or read or just...*be*.

Peace. Serenity. How often she had wished for that feeling over the past two years. Here, she could imagine regaining at least some of it.

Back at her hotel, she checked her bank account for the hundredth time, making sure the money was transferred and ready for the auction tomorrow, then she went to soak in the tub. She wound her long, dark hair up onto her head. *I really ought to get this cut*, she thought. Her hair hung down past her waist now; she hadn't been to a hairdresser since she didn't know how long. She risked a glance in the mirror, but then looked away again. Her dark eyes still had that haunted look she had grown accustomed to, but she could no longer bear to look at herself for long.

Hero Donati had been adopted at birth by an Italian-American businessman and his wife who already had one daughter, Imelda. Hero's birth mother had been a young Indian student at one of Milan's colleges who had become pregnant by her Italian lover and had given her child up for adoption, unable to care for the baby herself. From her mother, Hero had inherited a dark beauty—a beacon for so much male attention that Hero learned to deliberately downplay her appearance. She became intentionally tomboyish, wore thick-rimmed spectacles, and had remained resolutely single until she met Tom.

Tom, with his merry grey eyes and blonde hair, hadn't put the moves on her at all. Instead, they routinely sat together in classes at their college in Chicago and made fun of all the rich kids. Tom, working class from Wisconsin, had become her best friend, and then one night, her lover. They married the day after graduation, and Beth had been born a year later, the family settling in Chicago.

Hero had become a mother and wife, and to her shock, she loved it. Hero worked on her doctorate while raising Beth, and she and Tom had been blissfully happy together; even Hero's sometimes-fraught relationship with her adoptive family had improved. Beth was a radiant ball of utter joy and love, and even Hero's sister Imelda, who didn't have a maternal bone in her body, adored the young girl.

Three years, four months, and six days later, it all came to a brutal end. The family had been driving to Wisconsin to spend Christmas with Tom's family when a drunken driver slammed into their Volvo at high speed. Though three-year-old Beth was killed instantly, Tom lingered in a coma until pronounced brain-dead on day five. His parents had made the decision to turn off his life-support, because Hero couldn't; she was also in a coma and not expected to survive.

When she woke three months later, she wished she hadn't. Not one word could describe the depth of her heartbreak. Both her worried parents and Tom's bereaved parents tried to reach her, but no one could. On her behalf, they sued the drunk driver's employers and secured Hero a settlement just shy of eleven million dollars, but even so, Hero couldn't even begin to think about starting again.

For months, she stayed at home in the apartment she had shared with her husband and daughter and let life go on without her. Eventually, it took two incidents to shake her out of the fugue.

The first episode still seems unbelievable to Hero. One night, rather than sit home wrapped in Tom's sweater with Beth's favourite 'blankie' nuzzled next to her face, something snapped inside Hero. She put on her tightest dress and all her makeup and went out to a nightclub in the city. Drinking herself into a manic mood, dancing, making out with strangers, she fully intended to fuck someone just to numb the pain, but she chose wrong—so, so wrong. As soon as the man got her into his car, he turned violent, and Hero fought for her life, quickly escaping only after punching her attacker hard in the balls.

She caught a cab home, and inside her apartment, Hero spent the rest of the night alternating between sobbing and screaming.

One of her neighbors had called Imelda. "I think Hero needs you."

Imelda, who had never been an overly warm person, stripped Hero off and put her in the shower. Feeding her oatmeal, strong coffee, and sleeping pills, she put her adoptive sister to bed and stayed with her while she slept it off.

The next day, Hero dutifully listened to Imelda's harsh pep talk. Imelda didn't mince her words. "I don't care what you do, Hero, but do something. Go off on a world trek, open an art gallery, go teach in China. But you need to snap out of this. Tom and Beth are dead."

Hero had turned on her sister. "Do you think I've forgotten, Melly? I *know* they're fucking dead! I wish I were, too. Jesus."

Imelda regarded her coolly. "Then do it. Kill yourself. Be that selfish. Mom and Dad need that on top of losing Beth. Do it."

Hero had stared at her sister, dumbfounded. She knew Melly was just trying to shock her out her funk, but at that moment, she hated her sister. Hated. "I have to get out of this damn country."

"Good. Do it. Bye, now." Imelda had walked out, calling back over her shoulder. "And if I see you again, it'll be too soon."

Fucking bitch.

Hero was angry now, but her anger had become a cold, silent thing that ate away at her soul. She would escape. She would go back to Italy; she still held citizenship there, after all. Maybe she would try and find her mother or her father—her birth parents. Maybe. She just knew she couldn't stay in Chicago a moment longer.

Banishing those thoughts of the past as far as she ever managed to, Hero climbed out of the tub and headed to bed. Tomorrow she would bid for that small apartment in the Villa Patrizzi. She would win it. And then she would move into it. And maybe. Maybe. *Maybe* then she could restart her life.

CHAPTER TWO

The great terrace of the Villa D'Este in Cernobbio was packed with Lake Como's elite: the women gorgeous, the men handsome in their designer suits, as they drifted around, champagne in hand, socializing before the auction began.

There was only one lot in this auction and as Arturo arrived, he went to find the auctioneer and to shake his hand. "I'm looking forward to this, Claudio."

The older man nodded. "It certainly has the feel of an event, Signore Bachi. I have a feeling you will be a very happy man by the end of today."

As Arturo started toward Peter, who he could see across the room, he was frequently stopped by both attractive women and admiring men, all wanting a few moments of his coveted attention. By the time he finally reached Peter, who was rolling his eyes and smirking, Arturo's confidence was sky-high.

"Peter, my friend, this is a good day."

"Cautious optimism, Turo," Peter said, his Canadian stoicism at full power. Arturo grinned at his friend.

When they'd met at Harvard, they quickly found they had the same irreverent sense of humor. Peter had been the manwhore of the college, and he relished his role; Arturo had Flavia and was deliriously happy. It had been only after Flavia was murdered that Peter showed his serious and loyal side. He never left Arturo's side during the funeral and the subsequent murder investigation within which Arturo was a natural suspect. Luckily for him, he had a strong alibi; the reason he was late to the party that day was he had been helping a young mother change a burst tire in the pouring rain. The woman happened to be the daughter of the local newspaper owner, and when Arturo was questioned, she came forward immediately.

Peter Armley was a year older than Arturo, already forty and still resolutely single. Unlike Arturo, he was picky about who he slept with and always called them back, even if just to say goodbye. He was on good terms with most of his former girlfriends and had even dated a couple for significant periods of time. A tall man, an inch shorter than Arturo's six-six, Peter could easily pass as a Roman citizen wearing a toga and laurel wreath in the Coliseum. His handsome face looked to be hewn from rock, but when he smiled, his blue eyes shone with warmth. His close-cropped brown hair was always neat, and his suits were Saville Row.

A math genius, he was recruited by Philipo to be the company's financial director—and to look after Arturo's finances. Arturo teased his friend about being his 'accountant,' but it really was down to Peter's handling of the finances that Arturo was the man he was now.

"Listen," Arturo told his friend, "I just want you to know, that if everything goes well with this auction, it's entirely down to you, Pete. You picked me up out of the sinkhole. I love you, brother."

"My pleasure." Pete smiled and looked at his watch. "Twenty minutes."

Arturo nodded. "Gotta go pee before it kicks off. Hold my champagne."

He made his way into the villa and found the restroom on the second floor. It was quiet up here, and Arturo relaxed in the moment's peace before the auction started. Stepping out of the restroom, he made his way back towards the stairs and then stopped.

At the far end of the hallway, a woman was staring out of the window, her features in profile, and Arturo's heart nearly stopped. Her long, dark hair, falling in soft waves, was pulled over one shoulder, and she looked so sad it made Arturo's chest hurt. Her resemblance to Flavia was so uncanny that everything in Arturo's body screamed at him to go to her.

She was wearing a white dress that ended just above the knee; the dress molded to her body, her full breasts, the soft curve of her belly, the long legs. Seeming to sense his scrutiny, she suddenly looked up at him, and Arturo's chest tightened at the depth of sadness in her lovely, dark eyes. He wanted to know what was making this beautiful woman so unhappy and how to make her smile again.

"*Buongiorno,*" he said softly. She blinked at him, those big doe eyes a little startled at his speaking.

"*Buongiorno.*" A soft, American-accented voice. Her lips were plump, pink, and parted slightly, and Arturo felt his body respond, becoming aroused by this mysterious stranger.

They stared at each other for a long moment before she turned away. "*Scuzi.*" She disappeared back into the hotel, and Arturo stepped forward, ready to pursue her, but then he heard Peter's voice from the stairs.

"Turo? They're ready. Let's go."

Arturo hesitated, his heart still thumping hard again his chest. God...what a fucking beautiful woman...he *had* to know who she was.

"Turo? Come on. Hotel Bachi awaits."

A HALF HOUR LATER, Arturo was no longer thinking of the beautiful woman, nor was he in a good mood any longer. "How the fuck did that happen? It *did* happen, right?"

He'd been outbid. He, Arturo Bachi, had been *outbid*. The apartment was sold and not to him. He could feel the stares of his friends, colleagues, and investors as he tried to process what had just happened.

Bidding had started off as expected, somewhere in the low hundred-thousands and had quickly shot up to almost a million. Arturo had shot a smug look at Peter, then at George Galliano, who raised his champagne glass at him, somewhat sarcastically.

Then it had all gone to hell. Just as the auctioneer was about to bring down the hammer, there was a new bid. Two million. A hush ran through the crowd. Arturo rocked back in shock and scanned the attendees to see who the new bidder was, but he or she wasn't giving themselves away.

"Two-five," he shot back.

Three million.

Peter was looking alarmed, shaking his head at Arturo. The top end of their budget for the apartment was only one and half million, and in any case, the apartment was only worth a tenth of that.

"Four million," Arturo called it, and Peter made a disgusted noise.

"Turo, *no*."

Five million. Another, louder gasp in the crowd and a hum

of astonishment. Peter grabbed Arturo's arm as the auctioneer looked at him. "Signore Bachi?"

"Arturo, if you do this, I'm out. I mean it, I quit. You cannot do this. It's reckless, and you'll be humiliated. Whoever this is… obviously money is nothing to them. Let it go. We'll figure out something else."

Arturo stared at his friend helplessly. Peter wasn't kidding, but it was Arturo's dream that was slipping away.

"Signore Bachi?"

Everyone was staring at him. Peter's eyes were fierce, and finally Arturo shook his head, his heart sinking. "No."

Another hum of gossip, and then the hammer came down. "Sold for five million euros."

"To whom?"

"Yes, to whom?"

"Who bought it?"

The questions came thick and fast. The auctioneer held his hands up. "I'm sorry, my friends. This is a buyer who wishes to remain anonymous."

Arturo felt a rising anger. "They won't be anonymous for long," he said, grimly, and Peter sighed, mostly from relief.

"Let's get out of here, Turo. I'll buy you a drink."

On their way out, and despite his anger, the thought of the beautiful woman drifted through his mind again, and he looked around, disappointed when she was nowhere to be found. He could do with an angry fuck right now.

Even as he thought it, he felt a wash of shame. *No.* She wasn't someone he could forget the next morning. Something about her spoke to him in more than just desire; he felt connected with the deep sadness in her lovely face.

He was still thinking about her as he got into Peter's Lamborghini who drove them back to the bar in Como he and

Peter owned, and he found, strangely, his anger had dissipated quicker than he would have thought.

He had to see her again—that much Arturo knew. He had to see her again...and soon. Because more than anything now, on this day of disappointments, he wanted to see her smile.

CHAPTER THREE

Hero's hand shook as she signed the documents which would make her the owner of the Villa Patrizzi apartment. Five million euros. Holy hell. She'd had no idea she would go that high for what was essentially only four small rooms, but as the bidding went higher, it had become imperative that she secure it. It seemed impossible that she wouldn't.

Of course, that was when she saw who she was bidding against. *Him.* The man she had seen upstairs; the man whose physical beauty had sent her body into a frenzy of arousal after just one look. His green eyes, brooding and dangerous, his dark curls...his incredible body in that exquisite suit...*Jesus.* As they had stared at each other, all Hero could think of was what it would be like if he were to approach her, touch her, fuck her right there against the window. God, she had gotten wet even thinking about what was underneath his clothes.

And immediately she was ashamed. She'd never felt that way about anyone—even Tom. She had loved Tom with every cell in her body, but they had been best friends before they were lovers.

But the look in the man's eyes had been a mirror of her feelings, she could tell. She only had to say the words...*fuck me*...and she knew without a doubt, he would not have hesitated.

And she wanted to punish him for making her feel like that, making her feel so disloyal to Tom's memory, for taking that away from her. So, she bid a ridiculous amount to beat him to the apartment. And won. It was a Pyrrhic victory at best. Five million was a massive chunk of her settlement—and the apartment was definitely not worth it.

She pushed the thought away as she shook hands with the auctioneer. "Would it be possible for you to call me a cab, please?"

"Of course, Madam. Please wait here and make yourself comfortable."

Hero sat back and tried to steady her shaking hands. Maybe she'd go out to eat tonight, walk through the town, mingle with the tourists, try to feel like a human being again. The paperwork on the apartment would go through quickly now, and she would be able to move in by the end of the week.

Not that she had anything to move in apart from her clothes, her art supplies, and her books. She would have to find a record player somewhere and some vinyl: Ella Fitzgerald, Billie Holiday, maybe some Paolo Conti. She could see herself sitting out on the balcony overlooking the lake, her watercolor paints in front of her, listening to Billie. That, to Hero, was her idea of heaven. Maybe lunch: fresh bread, some cheese, a bag of sweet, juicy peaches. Cold white wine. The image was so appealing she found herself smiling to herself, and when the auctioneer came to tell her the cab was waiting, she found herself shaking his hand far more enthusiastically than she meant to.

Back at her hotel, she changed out of the form-fitting dress and back into her usual uniform of a grey-marl T-shirt and jeans. She glanced in the long mirror, noting that she should really try to dress better.

You look beautiful no matter what you wear. Tom's words came back to her.

Her eyes filled with easy tears, and she dashed them away impatiently. Stop wallowing. She should go out into the city now, do some window shopping or maybe *actual* shopping. *I have a new home. Time to get to know it.*

She grabbed her bag, slung it across her body, and left the hotel room.

IT WAS late by the time Peter left Arturo at the bar and went home. Arturo, buzzy on a few vodkas, sat outside at one of the small tables, smoking a cigar and people watching. People-watching *and* brooding over his loss today. *Damn it.* Peter had talked him down from bribing the auctioneer to tell him who had purchased the Villa Patrizzi apartment.

"Dude, don't be dumb. Wait a couple of weeks until the person moves in, then knock on the door."

"What if they have no intention of moving in? What if they just bought it to fuck with me?" An idea came then. "Fuck, I bet it was George."

Peter sighed. "Don't even go there, man. This feud you two have…it's gone on for far too long."

Arturo's eyes narrowed. "He fucked Flavia, Pete. He fucked my girlfriend and then told me about it after she'd been murdered."

Peter nodded, his blue eyes serious. "I know, Turo. But…we all lost Flav, too. You knew he had feelings for her—and admit it, you did flaunt it in front of him."

Arturo looked away from his friend's gaze. "I was young and stupid."

"And so was he."

Arturo shook his head. "It's gone too far now, Pete. Why did he have to tell me? I already had the image of Flavia, dead, gutted, and then he gave me another of the two of them together." His pleasant buzz wavered dangerously at the memory.

"Turo, stop," Peter warned. "Move on. George didn't buy the apartment. I saw him leave before the auction began."

Arturo sighed. "Fine. But he could have sent a proxy..." His friend's dark look finally broke through his moody, drunken haze. "Okay, I'll stop."

Peter looked at his watch. "Man, I have to go. I'll come over in the morning. We'll talk about what we do next."

So now Arturo rose from the table, throwing down money for the drinks, and took off into town. He wandered aimlessly around the side streets for a time, but as he turned down an alleyway to double back to his car, he caught sight of a woman walking in front of him. He enjoyed the sway of her hips, the curve of her waist, her rounded, perfect ass. She only wore a gray T-shirt and jeans, but the way she moved...

She stopped and turned to look into a bright shop window, and Arturo felt his pulse quicken as he saw her profile.

It was her. His white dress girl from the Villa D'Este. For a moment, he just watched her. God, she was beautiful—achingly, heartbreakingly so. He walked up behind her and met her gaze in the reflection in the window. He read so much in her lovely eyes: sadness, resignation—heat.

Neither of them spoke for a long moment. Then Arturo risked snaking his hand around her waist and letting his fingers stroke her belly through her T-shirt. Her eyes widened, and he paused, wondering if he'd made a terrible mistake and misread things completely. But then she leaned back into his body, and her hand crept around to cup his cock through his pants. Arturo groaned and pressed into her more intimately. He swept her hair to one side and pressed his lips to her neck.

She turned in his arms and gazed up at him, her eyes wary but full of desire. He stroked her cheek with his thumb. *"Bonne noche. I'm—"*

She cut him off with a swift, hard press of her lips to his.

"No names." Her voice was a low, gruff whisper, but it sent thrills through his body. He nodded and offered her his hand. She took it, only hesitating a little, and slowly he led her back to his car. He turned to her, confirming. "Yes?"

She nodded, and he opened the passenger door for her. *What are you doing, man? You don't even know her name!* But he hushed the inner voice and slid into the driver's seat. He gently brushed a lock of her hair over her ear. "Guess what we're going to do?"

A smile. At last, a smile. Small, hesitant, but a smile. He couldn't take his eyes off her exquisite face. He leaned in to kiss her again, lingering over it before starting the car and heading towards his villa.

4
CHAPTER FOUR

Hero, for the second time that day, couldn't stop trembling. *What the hell are you doing?* She asked herself over and over. So many feelings were rushing through her but none of them were as strong as the need to fuck this man. When he had appeared behind her, and she'd seen his eyes searching her face in her reflection, she had known what would happen.

When he had been so daring as to touch her belly—how the hell did he know it was her most sensitive erogenous zone?—she was lost. His lips were against her neck, and she felt herself wanting to touch him. His cock, twitching at her touch, was hot, thick, and long through his pants, and Hero quivered with desire.

Now, as he pulled his car up to the entrance of his villa, she could scarcely take anything in but the man beside her and the way he held her hand as they walked into the vast mansion, straight up the staircase to his bedroom. When he touched her again, drawing her into his arms and kissing her so passionately, her head swam.

"I'm going to fuck you so hard, beautiful one." His deep,

mellifluous voice sent shivers through her—God, this man was pure sex.

"Don't wait, please, fuck me now." She said breathlessly, and he grinned, triumphant. He pulled her T-shirt over her head and swiftly freed her breasts from her bra, taking her nipple into his mouth and sucking so hard she thought she might pass out from the pleasure.

Stopping only to whisk off her jeans and panties and lay her on the bed, the man stripped off his own clothing quickly. Hero couldn't take her eyes off his body: hard pecs, washboard stomach, and his cock, standing so thick and proud against his belly.

He smiled at her admiration, fisting the root of his cock. "This is all for you, sweet girl. Spread those beautiful legs for me and let me see your delicious cunt."

Hero did as he asked, and with a groan, he dropped between her knees and buried his face in her sex, licking and teasing her, lashing his tongue around her clit until it was rock hard, then dipping his tongue deep into her cunt until she was weeping with pleasure.

As she came, he slid a condom over his cock, moved to cover her body and thrust his straining length deep inside her, making her cry out. He pinned her hands to the bed, his eyes never leaving hers. "*Cosi bella, cosi bella...*" *So beautiful.*

There were so many emotions in his eyes as they made love that Hero felt like a stranger in her own skin, as if she had always been meant to meet this man, make love with him, be here tonight—spend this particular night with him.

Her orgasm hit her hard, and she arched her back, pressing her belly against his, her breasts against his chest. The man buried his face in her neck, kissing, sucking, biting at her skin as he groaned through his own climax, and she shivered as she felt him come. His lips trailed down her spine. "Excuse me for a moment, *bella.*"

She heard him go into the bathroom, obviously to deal with his condom, and she lay spent, her eyes closed, letting her body recover. She felt as if her skin were on fire, and when he came back to bed, the feeling of his fingertips stroking a circle around her navel made her eyes roll back in her head.

Arturo chuckled. "You have a very sensitive belly, pretty one." He slid his thumb into the deep hollow and began to finger-fuck it, making her moan with pleasure. He chuckled as she came again, sighing and laughing softly.

"God, what you do to me..." Her eyes were shining, and he was happy to see that the sadness in them was lessened.

"Tell me your name, lovely girl."

But she shook her head. "No names. This is perfect just the way it is."

"Then, let us call each other..." He cast around for two names, then spotted the book on his nightstand. "Beatrice and Benedict. From *Much Ado About Nothing*."

He was surprised when her face flamed red. "What?"

"Nothing. You like Shakespeare?"

He nodded. "Very much. You?"

"Some. I studied him at college, but I have to say, I prefer more modern writers."

Arturo smiled. "Such as?"

"McCarthy, Angelou, Arundhati Roy. Haruki Murakami."

Arturo smiled. "I'm also a fan of Murakami. Favorite book of his?"

"Kafka on the Shore."

"Same."

She looked skeptical, and he held his hands up. "I swear, *Principessa*."

"I'll believe you." They gazed at each other for a long time, then she raised her hand to his face and cupped his cheek. "You're really beautiful."

Arturo grinned, inclining his head. "Thank you."

She giggled at his confidence. "I forgot Italian men had no time for false modesty."

Arturo propped himself up on his elbow next to her. "Forgot? You don't live here?"

"I didn't. I just relocated here. I was born here, but I've spent most of my life in the States."

"Whereabouts?"

"Chicago."

He smiled. "Nice town." But he noticed the sadness was creeping back into her eyes. He bent his head and kissed her. "Beautiful girl, what is it? Why do you look so sad? What is your pain?"

She stared at him for a long time then sat up. "I have to go." She reached for her clothes and began to put them on.

Arturo was bemused by the sudden change in atmosphere. "Did I say something wrong? Or do something wrong?"

She shook her head, looking as if she were close to tears. "No." She stopped, hesitated and then pressed her lips to his for a second. "You're perfect," she whispered, leaning her forehead against his, closing her eyes. "But that's why I have to go."

He felt her tears on his cheek and cradled her face in his hands. "Don't go. Stay. Stay with me."

She shook her head. "I can't."

Arturo felt an ache in his chest. He didn't want this night to end, didn't want her to go away from him. "At least let me drive you back home."

She hesitated, those dark brown eyes wary but then nodded. "Thank you."

THEY DIDN'T SPEAK as he drove her back to her hotel, but Arturo held her hand, and she didn't pull away. At her hotel, he walked her to the door. "Can I call you?"

"I don't think that's a good idea. Tonight has been...a revelation. Please, let's leave it as perfect as it has been."

Unhappy, he took her in his arms and kissed her. "I will never forget you. If you change your mind...my name is Arturo Bachi. Everyone here knows me. You only have to call."

She kissed him again, lingering as if to memorize the feel of his lips against hers. "Goodbye, Arturo Bachi. I'll never forget you either."

Reluctantly, he let her go, watching her walk into the hotel and out of his life. He got back into the car and felt utterly bereft, even—he was astonished to find—a little heartbroken. She was the most amazing, sensual woman, and he wanted to know everything about her—and never let her go. He hadn't felt like this since Flavia...and maybe not even then. Guilt crept in, but he couldn't deny his feelings. His white dress girl, his 'Beatrice' had woken something in him he didn't think he'd ever felt before.

Arturo shook himself and started the car. As he drew away from the hotel, every meter he drove further away from her hurt more. But she had been clear—it wasn't meant to be.

"Fuck it," he said miserably, and pressed down hard on the gas pedal.

HE'D SEEN the girl at the auction, and his breath had been taken away. At first, he thought he was hallucinating. Flavia...but no, this girl was petite and curvy, whereas Flavia had been tall and willowy, and although he hated to admit it, this girl was even more achingly beautiful than Flavia.

He'd been absorbed in the auction at the time and hadn't seen her slip away. Imagine his surprise when he'd followed

Arturo through the streets of the town and watched as they'd found each other.

Following Arturo's Mercedes, he watched them go into the Villa Bachi, saw Arturo's bedroom light go on. They were fucking. Of course, they were. There wasn't a woman in Como that Arturo hadn't fucked; why would this girl be any different?

Because she was a newcomer. He could tell by the way she walked through the town, studying everything as if it were new. He wondered if she had family close or friends. When Arturo had driven her back to her hotel, he followed her into the hotel, heard her ask the receptionist for the key to Room 45.

Room 45. That was good to know. He wondered how long she was staying, how much time he had to carry out his plan.

He so wanted to see Arturo's face when they called him to tell him his beautiful one-night stand was dead. To see his grief when they told him she'd been killed in the exact same way as his beloved Flavia twenty years ago.

5
CHAPTER FIVE

"Where the *hell* are you?" Imelda's already strident voice echoed through the speakerphone in Hero's room. Hero, dressing, rolled her eyes.

"What do you care, Melly? You told me to go off by myself."

"I didn't mean it, you know that. God, Hero, we've been worried sick."

Hero had to raise her own voice to make Imelda listen. "I'm in Italy. Lake Como."

There was a pause on the end of the line, and when Imelda spoke again, her voice was calmer. "Oh. Good."

"I'm doing what you told me, going 'Wild' like Reese Witherspoon, but instead of hiking, I'm hanging out with the Clooneys. Satisfied?"

"You've met George and Amal?"

"No, doofus, I'm just saying. I picked a place on the map, and it's here." She paused for effect. "I bought an apartment."

"What?"

Hero was smugly satisfied with her sister's stunned response. "Tell me you just did a comedy jaw-drop, Melly. Please tell me you did that."

"Stop messing around, Hero. Did you really buy a house, or are you just yanking my chain again?"

Hero sighed. "No, I really did. I think I pissed off some rich muckety-muck who had his eye on it, too. I outbid him." *That rich muckety-muck, by the way, Imelda, whose cock drilled me to his bed last night and whose kiss I can't stop thinking about.*

Again, Imelda was silent. Hero, tugging on her socks, listened to the sound of her sister's breathing. "Mel?"

"Well," her sister's voice was softer now, "that's very positive. Nesting. Making a home. What are you going to do there?"

"Read, write, paint, enjoy the view, eat everything in sight, get as fat as all get-out."

"All good things."

Hero's eyebrows shot up. Usually, if Mel saw Hero had put on even a pound, she had her in the gym before she did anything else. "Lots of carbs, Mel."

"I know you're just trying to make me crazy, but seriously, I think this will be good for you."

Another long silence. "You know, you could always come visit, Melly."

Hero waited for her sister's response and was surprised when she said, "You know what, Hero? I might just take you up on that."

Hero was stunned. She and Imelda had never been close, never been the sort of—adoptive—siblings who hugged each other or visited regularly. Imelda's visits had been even less since Beth died, although she still managed to harangue Hero by phone regularly. Hero felt a strange shift in their relationship now.

"You are always welcome, Melly. *Always.*"

Her sister cleared her throat. "I'll call you soon. Don't disappear again."

And the phone went dead. "And goodbye to you, too." Hero

dumped her phone in her bag. Today she was going to spend all day out of the hotel, not because she had any particular place to go, but because she was terrified that Arturo Bachi would turn up at the hotel to find her—and she didn't have the strength to resist him.

She closed her eyes now and relived the previous night: his hands on her body, his lips against her skin, his huge cock thrusting ever deeper inside her...she shivered with pleasure. That the man was an expert in bed was undeniable; he knew exactly what she liked without even asking, her body completely under his control. She could get lost in those eyes of his...

"Stop it." She opened her eyes and took a deep breath in, pushing all thoughts of Arturo away. She knew men like him. Arrogant, rich, thinking they could buy anything they wanted. Yes, he'd clearly wanted her, and yes, he'd had her—but only because she had wanted him, too, at least for a night.

Those wild, dark curls, that hard body...

"Nope, nope. Nope." Besides, when he found out it was she who'd outbid him at the auction, he'd certainly lose any desire to be friendly towards her.

Hero pulled on her Chuck Taylors and grabbed her purse, strapping it across her body, and grabbed the room key. She would go out, find somewhere to buy art supplies, and have a look around for furniture for the apartment.

She would not, she told herself, not think of Arturo Bachi for one more second. She wouldn't. She really wouldn't...

ARTURO FOUND himself preoccupied as he sat in a meeting with Peter and the board members. He kept thinking of her soft hair, her pink lips, the fresh scent of her skin, the way her clit tasted in his mouth...

Peter nudged him. "Turo? What do you think?"

"Of what?"

Peter glared at him. "Ludo is making a proposal."

Arturo looked apologetically at the older man. "Ludo, forgive me, I'm sorry. Could you repeat the question?"

Ludo, an old friend of Arturo's father, smiled kindly at him. "The hotel. I'm proposing we renovate the apartments in the Villa Patrizzi and then sell them as separate units. We should see some profit, and then we can use that to seek out another property to turn into the hotel."

Arturo shook his head. "No. I want the Patrizzi. We need to get that apartment."

Peter sighed. "Turo...we simply do not have the budget to buy the purchaser out."

"*Mio Dio!*" Arturo exclaimed in frustration. "It's only five million! I'll put it in myself."

"No."

Arturo narrowed his eyes at his best friend. "And you'll stop me how?"

Peter met his friend's gaze steadily. "I can't. But if that happens...I'm gone. Turo, I mean it. This is not what this conglomerate agreed to. We all put in the same amount of cash; we all take the same risks; we all reap the same rewards. That agreement is watertight. Five million for one apartment is nonsense, and we don't have to make the same mistake as that buyer. What Ludo is proposing is the best way forward."

Arturo sat in silence before glancing around the room. He could tell the others agreed with Peter, and he knew his best friend was right. Still...

"Fine. I'll begin the search for some new premises."

He saw Peter visibly relax. *Good. Let him think he'd won.*

But Arturo knew in his bones, Villa Patrizzi would one day be the site of his dream hotel. If the apartment's buyer wouldn't sell to him, then there were other ways to force them to sell or to quit the place.

Arturo hid a smile. He was going to make their life hell—and his business partners were going to help do that, whether they knew it or not.

HERO WAS aware of the man gazing at her as she sat outside the café. She shot a look at him, and he smiled at her, friendly and warm. She looked away, and then sighed as she saw him out of the corner of her eye, get up to approach her.

Just leave me alone.

But she had been raised to be polite, and when he was by her side, she looked up and gave him a pleasant smile. "Hello."

"*Bueno giorno, signorina.* George Galiano."

She shook the offered hand. "Hero Donati."

George indicated the other seat at her table. "May I sit for a moment?"

Hero stifled a sigh and nodded. "Please."

He was tall, not as tall as Arturo, but broad-shouldered and slim-hipped. His brown hair was short and neatly styled, his beard trimmed and shaped. His dark brown eyes searched hers. "I hope you don't think I'm intruding, but I believe I saw you at the auction yesterday. For the Patrizzi apartment?"

"Yes, I was there."

George chuckled lightly. "It was quite the scandal. That apartment was expected to go to Arturo Bachi. We all expected it to go to him, but then, as you saw, a mysterious buyer swooped in and snapped it up. After the auction, I saw you going into the auctioneer's office. Coincidence, yes?"

Hero sipped her coffee. "Mr. Galiano, do you have a question you want to ask me?"

"You bought the apartment."

"Yes." She didn't see how it was his business, but she wasn't going to lie.

George's handsome face split with a wide grin. "Then, Miss Donati, I owe you a drink."

That stumped her. "I take it you and Mr. Bachi are not friends?"

"Not any longer. Excuse me." He addressed the nearby waiter. "Could we have some champagne?"

GEORGE GALIANO WAS CHARMING to be certain, but Hero wouldn't trust him in any situation. Still, as far as a pleasant acquaintance went, he was certainly easy on the eye and amusing to talk to. His rancor towards Arturo, she discovered, went deep.

"We were friends," he said, "a long time ago." He sighed, regretfully. "We were in the unfortunate position of being in love with the same woman, and it didn't end well for any of us."

"So, now you hate each other?"

"For my part, it isn't hate. Only too much has passed between us for us ever to go back."

Hero felt a little uncomfortable. "But you're glad he lost the apartment?"

"Call me petty, but yes. Arturo has had too much influence in this town for far too long. It was time he was taken down a peg or two."

"That's not why I bought the apartment. I had no idea Arturo Bachi even existed before yesterday." *Although I sure found out who he was last night...*

A giggle bubbled up, and she hurriedly covered it with a cough. George didn't seem to notice. "So, you are staying in our lovely town?" he asked.

"For the foreseeable future, yes."

He smiled. "Then perhaps you would allow me to show you around sometime?"

Hero hesitated, then nodded. "Perhaps."

"Good." He drained his champagne and reaching for her hand, kissed the back of it. "If you will excuse me, lovely lady, I have a meeting to get to. It was good to meet you."

"You, too."

Hero watched him walk away, getting into a chrome-clad Bentley. *Flashy.* That was the sense she got from him, and although Arturo also flaunted his wealth, Hero got the impression that he was a little less...what? Ostentatious?

She sighed. Who cared? It wasn't as if she had any reason to be involved with either of these men anymore. She drained her coffee, left her untouched champagne on the table, and rose to walk around the town.

SHE HAD ABSOLUTELY no idea of the effect she had on men, he decided. He walked a few yards behind her with other people strolling between them, but he could see male heads turning as she passed by. Her long hair was pulled up into a messy bun at the nape of her neck and her outfit was an obviously well-loved, fraying T-shirt and blue jeans that clung to her shapely hips and legs. She was stunning.

Flavia had been equally beautiful, but far younger—only eighteen—when he'd killed her.

He still remembered everything about that night and how perfectly he planned it. It was a costume party at the Villa Charlotte. She'd agreed to meet him outside at the gate leading to the lake. She had been dressed as a wood nymph, her dress floating around her and her beauty enhanced by the moonlight. The perfect 'O' of her mouth as he slid the knife into her. The horror and pain in her eyes. He'd held her as she bled out in his arms.

Ssh, ssh, my pretty one. It's all over now...

She hadn't spoken, but the 'Why?' was in her eyes.

Because you loved him...

Her eyes closed for the last time as the last of her blood pumped from the many stab wounds, and he had quietly set her adrift on the lake, looking like Ophelia: her body soaked in her blood, her hair streaming about her head.

Damn it. His cock was hard again. *Control,* he told himself sharply. It'd been twenty years since Flavia, and now it was time to remind Arturo Bachi that anytime he dared to fall in love, he would lose everything until one day he'd get the message.

He had no idea if Arturo would fall in love with this new girl, but he sensed that something was different about her—something special. He hoped Arturo would fall in love with this beautiful woman.

Because it would make it so much more satisfying when he killed her.

CHAPTER SIX

As she was drying off after her shower, Hero heard a soft knock on the door and knew instinctively who it was. She'd been imagining him as she'd stood in the steamy heat, picturing his hard, naked body wrapped around her from behind...

Wrapping the towel around herself, she walked over to the door and asked, "Who is it?"

"Arturo, principessa. Forgive me. I couldn't stay away."

Smiling, Hero opened the door and looked up at him. "Hello again." He was wearing a navy sweater and blue jeans and looked boyish and beautiful.

For a second, she just stared at him, then stood aside to let him in. As he moved past her, she closed the door behind him and then deliberately let her towel drop. Arturo groaned.

"*Bellissimo...*" He dropped to his knees and gripped her hips, pulling her directly into him, and Hero went willingly. "*Bella, bella, bella.*"

His low voice reverberated against her clit, and she moaned softly as his tongue lashed around it. There was something so erotic about being naked while he was still dressed. Arturo tumbled her to the bed, pushed her knees to her chest, hooking her ankles over his shoulders, and took his time to go down on her. His fingers bit into the flesh of her thighs, his tongue was relentless as he brought her to orgasm, leaving her breathless and panting.

His mouth moved up to find her nipples as he unzipped his fly. She helped him free his cock, stroking the length of it before guiding him inside. God, she wanted him so badly. She clung to him as they fucked, each thrust harder and more ferocious. They were clawing at each other like animals, the bed shifting under their movements, the headboard banging relentlessly on the wall, but neither cared.

Their need for each other was feral. Arturo fucked her into the most glorious orgasm of her life, and Hero screamed out his name, again and again, delirious with pleasure. He fucked her again on the floor, then once more in the shower, and when he came, he pumped thick creamy cum deep inside her belly, and she arched her back, pressing her breasts against his chest.

They didn't speak. Their lovemaking went on into the early hours, and by the time he kissed her goodbye, she was exhausted but satisfied. She almost asked him to stay but knew it would be a mistake.

Still, when he pressed his lips to hers and whispered, "Tomorrow?" she nodded, knowing she would need her fix of him again.

It was only later, when she was alone, that she realized they'd forgotten to use a condom.

ARTURO DROVE HOME, smiling. God, she was intoxicating, and now he knew her name. *Hero.* Hero Donati. No wonder she'd been bemused when he'd named them 'Beatrice and Benedict' from *Much Ado About Nothing.* He'd been so close to the truth, only one character away. He hated leaving her at the hotel; he wanted her in his bed always, but he knew he had to tread carefully. She was clearly a flight risk.

At home, he opened his laptop and typed her name into the search engine. Nothing. He added 'Chicago' and pressed Enter. He would have missed the entry entirely if he hadn't scrolled down the page. A death notice.

THOMAS AND BETH LAMBERT, *beloved husband and daughter of Hero D. Lambert. Funeral to be held at St. Maria of Sacred Heart, Thursday, 5th January. No flowers, please. Donations to Chicago Children's Hospital.*

A SHOCK RAN THROUGH ARTURO. She had been married? Had a child? Reeling with the shock, he searched further until he found the newspaper report.

FATHER AND DAUGHTER *Killed in Horror Smash.*

CHICAGO: *A father and daughter were killed Christmas Eve when a drunken driver crashed into their Toyota in heavy snow at Kenosha. Schoolteacher Thomas Lambert, 30, and his three-year-old daughter, Beth, were fatally injured, with the child pronounced dead at the scene. Mr. and Mrs. Lambert were transported to the nearest emergency room where Mr. Lambert died five days after the crash. His wife, Hero Lambert, 26, remains in a coma in critical condition. The driver's blood alcohol content was found to be five times the legal limit.*

. . .

A DRUNK DRIVER. In one second, Hero's life was destroyed. Arturo felt sick and a little guilty for invading her privacy. If she had wanted him to know...

No. He just wouldn't tell her what he knew; that was best for now. If his plan to seduce her worked, then he would let her tell him in her own time.

He closed his eyes. The thought of Hero, lying in the wreck of a car, screaming for her lost husband, her darling daughter, made his chest hurt.

She looks so much like Flavia...is that the reason? He shook his head, sighing, and closed the laptop. Comparing the two women would not help matters.

He went to bed, hoping to get a couple of hours of sleep before he had to go to work, but his dreams were troubled with an image of Flavia's dead body floating away from him, and his Hero, his lovely Hero, being stabbed to death in front of him by Flavia's killer.

IN A FOUL MOOD because of his nightmares, Arturo went into his office, stalking down the hallway right past his assistant's desk without saying anything.

"Peter called." Marcella followed him into his office, used to ignoring his moods. "He says he's found a few promising options for the new hotel. He wants to know if you just want to put the Patrizzi apartments straight back on the market as is or go ahead with the refurbishments."

Arturo sat down heavily in his chair. "Tell Pete to call me, please. I want to refurb the whole place. Might as well make some profit off it."

"Thank you. By the way...good morning."

Arturo did smile then. "Good morning, Marcella."

"Grouch."

"You're fired."

Marcella grinned. "Want coffee?"

"Yes, please."

"Well, you know where the coffee pot is."

Arturo laughed. American-born Marcella had worked with him for years and had been his confidante and his friend—almost his sister. When he got too arrogant, she would just stare at him, do the pencil-tapping thing, until he backed down. She told him to fuck off to his face when he was rude to her; she brought him hot tea and pastries when he was down.

"Marcie...can I ask you something?"

Marcella, who was halfway out of the door, stopped and studied him. "Work or pleasure?"

"Pleasure."

"Ooh, gossip. Ask away." She flopped into the chair opposite him and crossed her long legs.

Arturo cleared his throat. "I met someone."

Marcella's eyes opened wide. "No. *Way*."

Arturo held up his hands to forestall her excitement. "It's complicated."

Marcella sighed. "When isn't it with you? Did you fuck her yet?"

Arturo looked away sheepishly.

"*Turo*." Marcella stretched out his name, berating him. "Woo a girl first. I know that monster in your pants has a mind of its own, but jeez..." She laughed but then looked at him, her eyes serious. "Do you like her?"

"I do. But I don't even know her—rather, she doesn't want me to know anything. I...might have gleaned some facts on my own."

"Stalker."

"I don't want to invade her privacy or overstep her boundaries. But I did find out something pretty major about her. Should I tell her that I know?"

Marcella shook her head. "No. That would freak her out, believe me. We women live in a world where any...invasion... however well-meaning or sweet...could mean something bad. Something like violence. So, no, Arturo, don't tell her. If she wants you to know, she'll tell you."

"Thanks, Marcie."

"Who is she?"

"That," he said, nodding, "is what I intend to find out."

THREE THINGS HAPPENED in a very short space of time that morning. Hero found a pharmacy and bought a box of condoms. They'd left it unsaid, but if Arturo turned up at her door again tonight, she knew she wouldn't be able to resist him. She considered a pregnancy test, but it was way too soon for that. Of course, she would have to find a doctor to test for STDs, and she berated herself. How stupid was she to have risked her health for a quick—albeit spectacular—fuck?

The second thing was her realtor called and told her the paperwork for the apartment had gone through. "Congratulations. You can move in whenever you want."

Hero thanked her and told her she'd be in to pick up the keys that afternoon. "I hear you've pissed off Arturo Bachi," the realtor said with a chuckle. "Good. He deserves it."

Hero swallowed hard. "You know him?"

"Oh, I know him. He might pretend not to know me, but *I* know him."

So, Arturo had slept with her realtor. Great. Hero thanked her again and ended the call. What the hell was she doing? She had been in town less than a week, and already she had screwed one of the biggest man-whores around.

But she couldn't stop thinking about him, and she found that her guilt over 'betraying' Tom's memory grew less and less. He'd want her to be happy, right? It didn't mean Hero didn't miss her husband every single moment, because she did. But moving to Italy was supposed to be a new beginning in every way.

Hero pushed all thoughts aside and went to the art shop she had found on her travels yesterday. The store was empty except for the proprietor, a young woman about Hero's age, whose tightly curled hair was piled on top of her head. She grinned at Hero. "Hello again. Couldn't stay away?"

Hero smiled at her. The woman had an English accent, and her name badge read FLISS. She was small, tinier even than Hero, and she wore a 50s-style tea dress with pink flamingos on a turquoise background. Hero liked her immediately.

"I was window-shopping yesterday. Today I'm intending to spend money."

Fliss laughed. "Good to hear. What are you looking for?"

"Everything."

Over the next hour, Fliss showed her around the store, and Hero immersed herself in picking out fat, round pastels in every color, a set of professional watercolor half-pans, and pencils in every hardness. She and Fliss talked about their mutual love of art—like Hero, Fliss was the product of art college.

"I was doing my doctorate, but that's on hold for the moment." Hero told her, and Fliss looked interested.

"Listen, it's been a while since I got to talk about art like the geek I am. I'm closing for lunch in ten. Want to grab a bite to eat?"

Hero smiled. "I'd love that."

FLISS TOOK her to a small trattoria down a small alley. "This is one of Como's best-kept secrets," she said in a low voice. "The tourists don't know about it. It's cheap, but my God, the food is so, so good. I recommend the rabbit stew with polenta."

Over lunch—and Hero took Fliss's advice and almost swooned when she put the first delicious bite into her mouth—they shared their stories.

Fliss had moved to Lake Como after a school trip when she was young. "I swore that I would do everything in my power to be able to live here. I got lucky. My parents are reasonably well-off and gave me my first capital to start my business. When I told them I wanted to bring it over here, their first reaction was, "Oh, great, when can we visit?"

Hero smiled, feeling a little envious. "Have you got any siblings?"

"Three brothers, all older, all a major pain in my arse. They're all scientists. Can you believe it? But," and she leaned forward conspiratorially, "I was the only one to graduate with first-class honors."

Hero laughed. For the first time in forever, she felt like more than a jaded twenty-eight-year-old who had already been a wife, a mother, and a widow. For once, she felt...relaxed.

"Damn, look at that man."

Hero blinked and turned towards where Fliss was looking. A man was dumping an armful of papers onto a stand, and Arturo Bachi's face was on the front of each one. Hero's Italian was good enough to read the headline. *"Bachi Upset at Patrizzi Sale!"*

Whoops. She turned back to Fliss who was eyeing Arturo's picture with lustful glee. "Do you know him?"

Fliss shook her head. "No, but I hear stories. He's quite the wonder schlong."

Hero felt her face burn, and Fliss saw her expression. "You okay?"

"I'm good. Listen, I've had a great time. Can we do this again?"

Fliss grinned. "You bet."

They swapped numbers, and Hero found her way to her realtor's office. With a swell of excitement, she picked up the keys to her new home.

"Now, you know it's not furnished, right?" her realtor reminded her.

Hero nodded. "I know. I won't actually be living there until my furniture is delivered, so if you need me and my cellphone is off, please call the hotel."

SHE WAS SHAKING as she walked up to the top floor and paused before unlocking the door. Had she done the right thing spending all that money? Why had she been so determined to beat Arturo? Had it been just her attempt to show she still had some control over her life?

Hero took a deep breath, opened the door, and all her doubts fell away.

She was home.

CHAPTER SEVEN

Arturo called her this time.

"I thought I'd do things properly for a change," he chuckled. "Would you like to have dinner with me?"

Hero, walking back from the Patrizzi, smiled. "I'd love to. Where did you have in mind?"

"It's a surprise. Wear something slinky...and easy to take off."

She was still laughing when they said goodbye. Whether she admitted it or not, Arturo Bachi wasn't just a spectacular lover, he had a sense of fun, too, that she found appealing. She wondered if he would be very angry if she told him the truth about the apartment.

Feigning ignorance wasn't an option. The fact he wanted the apartment was well-known, even to her after only ten minutes spent at the auction house that day. No, she would have to come clean, give him her reasons why she bought the place and paid such an outrageous sum for it.

Dang it. As much as she hated lying to him, she also didn't want this to end. She craved his body—he was like a heady mix of sugar and heroin in her system.

Walking back to the hotel, still a block away, she became

aware that there was no one else on the street. The evening was dark with a cool breeze blowing up from the lake. As she walked, she heard the echo of footsteps behind her, and her gut twisted a little in apprehension. She stole a look behind her. A few steps behind her, a man, tall and broad-shouldered, followed. He was in shadow. It was probably nothing, but Hero slowed her pace and then stopped.

The man behind her stopped. Oh, shit...he *was* following her. She turned to face him. "What do you want?"

A second later, she regretted stopping when she saw a flash of steel in his hand. *Oh God no...* Hero turned and took flight towards the people she could see milling about in the town square.

With relief, she darted into the hotel, breathless as she asked for her key. The receptionist gave her a strange look, but Hero just shook her head. It was just a mugger, she thought to herself. But she was shaken.

She pushed open the door to her room, and at first, she didn't notice the envelope that must have been pushed under her door. When she did, she picked it up off the carpet, opened it and read,

You look beautiful today. It's a pity I'm going to kill you.

SHE DROPPED the letter as if it were scalding hot. What the actual hell? She sat on the edge of the bed, shaking. Who wanted to kill her? She was new in town for chrissakes, and the only person she could have any beef with would be...

No. She refused to believe Arturo Bachi was capable of hurting anyone, much less her. If he'd wanted to kill her, he would have done it that first night when no one had seen him take her home. He could have killed her, dumped her body in the lake, and gone on about his day. No.

But who else could it be? She didn't know anyone else—and she was pretty sure Fliss wasn't a crazy killer. Besides, the guy that followed her just now was huge. That made her feel sick. There was no way she'd be able to fight back against a killer that size. She tried to control her trembling in order to get dressed. She slipped into a lilac dress and fastened a gold chain around her neck, but she moved automatically, not really focusing on her appearance.

For the first time, she wondered if she had done the right thing by coming here. It just didn't make sense that someone had targeted her so quickly.

IN THE CAR with Arturo an hour later, she studied him carefully. "Where are we going?"

Arturo grinned over at her, and she could see no malice in his eyes. "A surprise."

His smile made her belly quiver, but her nerves were still frayed, and he seemed to notice. He reached over and took her hand. "Are you okay?"

She didn't answer for a moment and then said, "Hero. My name is Hero."

Arturo grinned sheepishly. "I know. I admit I saw the key card holder with your name written on it. Not Beatrice."

So, he was honest. Did it mean he was innocent? He was the only person who would have reason to hate her, and yet he was so caring, his eyes so full of desire for her.

He drove them to a small compound where a helicopter waited. Arturo helped Hero out of the car and then led her to the aircraft, still grinning and not telling her where they were going. He got into the pilot's seat, and Hero had to admit that she was impressed.

It also made her feel better that plenty of people had seen them take off together. Witnesses.

Stop it. He's done nothing wrong. Hero pulled in a deep lungful of air and tried to relax. Arturo reached over and stroked her face. "Okay?"

She nodded and turned her head to press her lips against his palm. Arturo smiled, leaning over to kiss her mouth.

The helicopter ride was exhilarating, and when they began to see city lights beneath them, Arturo said, "Milan. I thought you should see it at night."

A thrill went through her. Milan…she'd never been to the city and now as he landed the craft on top of a hotel, she felt as if she were walking in a dream.

The restaurant was exclusive and expensive, and they were led to a private booth in the back. "I thought we could talk without people listening in," Arturo said, bending to kiss her cheek. He was holding her hand, his fingers entwined in hers, and Hero felt a warmth surge through her. There was no way he was that good an actor to fake this affection. *No way.*

They sat side-by-side in the booth, and after the waiter took their order, Arturo put his arm around her and drew her closer. "That dress, the color is incredible next to your skin." He drew the back of his finger down her cheek.

He picked up her necklace, trailing his fingers along the chain, then letting them drift down her torso to her belly. Hero gave a tiny moan of desire. Arturo nuzzled her neck, "Sweet Hero…I have a suite booked at the Mandarin Oriental. I would be delighted if you would stay the night with me there. No pressure. One word from you and I'll cancel the room. Will you stay?"

Hero nodded, lost in his eyes. "Yes," she said in a scratchy voice, husky with an almost feral desire for him—and because she knew without a doubt that it would be their last night together. She wanted to have this last night to remember being in his arms, being fucked by him, because she knew one thing for sure: she was falling for him and that meant she had to tell him the truth.

And after that, she was certain Arturo would want nothing more to do with her. The thought of that was killing her.

ARTURO OPENED the door of the suite and stepped back to allow Hero in. God, she was so beautiful he could cry, but ever since dinner, where neither of them ate very much, she had been quiet. Was she nervous about staying with him? He hoped not.

Locking the door behind him, he went to where she stood staring out the floor-to-ceiling windows that overlooked Milan. The back of her dress was cut low revealing a heavenly expanse of honey-colored skin, and he trailed his finger down her spine. "You are perfect," he whispered, then pressed his lips to her bare shoulder. Hero reached around and cupped his cock in her hand, stroking him through his pants. He pulled at the tied halter of her dress, and the garment slithered to the floor. She wore no bra; her full, ripe breasts were perky, the nipples small and dark red. He moved so he could take each one in his mouth in turn, teasing each until it was rock hard. Hero stroked his hair as he did, both of them moving slowly and savoring each moment. He slid his hand between her legs and caressed her through her damp panties.

"You're wet."

"For you," she whispered, meeting his gaze. "Always for you."

He had to have her then, her words spurring the animal in him to erupt. He swept her onto the bed and stripped his own clothes off, swiftly rolling a condom down over his engorged, almost painfully hard cock and thrusting into her. Hero wrapped her legs tightly around his waist, her fingernails digging into his buttocks as she pulled him deeper and harder. Arturo kissed her with such ferocity he could taste blood, his hand moving to pin one of hers over her head. She came over and over as they fucked, and she begged him to never stop.

He locked his elbows, gazing down into her eyes. "Don't worry, my precious Hero, I'll never stop…never…" He thrust hard as he came, groaning her name, taking her mouth hungrily. "You're so beautiful, so lovely, *bella, bella bella*…" He knew, without a doubt, that he was in trouble, that he could easily fall in love with this woman, and if he did…God, his heart was still so fragile, so fearful that someone would take her away from him. He felt that dread so keenly tonight, but he didn't know why.

It was a perfect night: the flight, the meal, and now here he was making love with her, away from the gossips in Como, away from his responsibilities. She brought that out in him, or she had over the last few days, and he had to remind himself that they really didn't know anything about each other. She had finally told him her name, and he knew enough to realize that was a big step for her.

He wouldn't be the man who pressured her, especially after what she had been through in her young life. All he wanted to do was be with her, acutely aware that this was a complete one-eighty shift in his whole philosophy. The last three days had been a revelation to him.

Later, when she fell asleep, he slipped out of bed and snagged his phone from his jacket. Closing the bedroom door, he went into the living room of the suite and called Pete. "Hey, buddy, did I wake you up?"

Peter chuckled. "No, Turo. What's up?"

Arturo sighed. "I got trouble."

"What? What happened? Did you something stupid, Turo?"

"Maybe. It's a girl, Peter. I'm in love."

8
CHAPTER EIGHT

Arturo, I'm the one. I'm the one who smashed your dream. I'm the one who outbid you, bought the Patrizzi apartment. I knew you were bidding, and I went all out to beat you. I'm the one.

HERO KEPT GOING through what she would say as she dressed the next morning. She had intended to tell Arturo when they woke, but he had kissed her so sweetly, and his eyes had been so full of...love? That's what it had looked like, and she had been silenced. They had made love tenderly at first, and then, as Arturo started to goof around, they fucked in every room in the suite, laughing and playing, Arturo chasing her around the rooms until she gave up.

Then, when his cock was buried deep inside her, she couldn't think of anything else but him, his body, his smile, his mouth on hers. He would switch from tender to almost rough as he took her, but she gave as good as she got, tugging on his hair, biting his nipples, digging her nails into his back and his butt hard until he moaned. As they showered together, they compared battle scars: the grazes and bruises on each other from their lovemaking. He fucked her in the shower, easily holding her up against cold tile as his cock drove in and out of her swollen and sore cunt.

Her thighs ached, her breasts tingled, and her heart felt as if it had unfurled in her chest. She couldn't do it; she couldn't ruin this perfect time with this beautiful man. She would keep her secret for a little while longer.

She felt his arms snake around her waist, and his hand slip beneath her dress to stroke her belly. "Hey."

She leaned back into him, turning her head to kiss his mouth. "Hey."

Arturo gazed down at her, his eyes serious. "Is it wrong that I don't want this to end?"

Her stomach dropped. "This?"

"This trip, this city, with you."

She turned in his arms and locked hers around his waist. He nuzzled her nose with his own. "Hero..."

The way he whispered her name made it sound like the most bewitching sound in the world. "Arturo...I have something to tell you."

"Okay."

She swallowed. "I..." *Tell him. Get it over with now. Offer to give him the apartment. Beg him to forgive you.* "I...used to be married."

Arturo's eyes were sympathetic. "Would you be mad if I told you I knew?"

That stopped her. "What?" What the hell? Did he have a private detective on her? Did he already *know* about the apartment?

Arturo's arms tightened around her. "I see what you're thinking, and I swear, just the results of a Google search. I was curious."

Hero breathed out. Okay, that was normal at the beginning

of modern relationships, right? *But you didn't think of finding out about his story like that, did you?* "Okay, that's fine. Then you know."

"About your husband and daughter. I do, and I cannot tell you how sorry I am, my darling. Come sit. Let's really talk. I've ordered breakfast."

Over breakfast she told him about Tom and Beth, and to her surprise, it was easy to talk to him, and it felt good to really reminisce honestly about her grief, her love for Tom, and her darling Beth, her light.

"She really was the most amazing kid," she said, her eyes filling with tears. "I know every mom says that but, my God, I couldn't believe this incredible little creature came from me."

"Do you have a photo?"

She dug around in her purse and brought out two photos. One was just of Beth, yelling a banshee cry into the camera, grinning wildly. The other was all three of them: Tom encompassing his family in his arms as they smiled, not at the camera but at each other.

Arturo studied them both. "Wow. Wow. She looks just like you."

Hero felt a lump in her throat when Arturo used the present tense. "She...does." The tears escaped then, and she began to sob. Arturo folded her in his arms and just held her until she cried herself out.

When she finally pulled away, she felt lighter and surprisingly unembarrassed. Arturo smiled at her and stroked the back of his fingers down her face. "Sweet one, your daughter will always be with you. And your husband..." He looked back at the photo of Tom, and for a second, Hero couldn't read his expression. "He looks like a great guy."

"He was. He was my best friend." She sighed. "It was just... everything changed on a dime, you know? One second we were in the car singing pop songs and the next minute... gone. So final." She looked away for a moment until he turned her face gently back to his.

"I'm glad you told me. I want to know you, Hero."

Hero squeezed his hand. "What about you?"

"Me? You know me. My reputation precedes me."

"Arturo."

He shrugged. "There has been no one special in my life for years."

She looked at him curiously. "So, there was someone, once?"

The pained look on his face was so fleeting that she wondered if she'd imagined it, but then he was talking again, and she dismissed it.

"I'm a walking cliché, Hero," he said bluntly. "I'm arrogant as hell, and I sleep around. *Slept* around. Three days ago, I met the woman that one day I hope to marry."

That floored her...and frightened her. "Arturo...a marriage is more than great sex."

"I know. Or rather, I don't, but I hope to find out." He held her gaze steadily. Hero felt her heart beating way too hard against her ribs, and she got up.

"Don't make fun of me."

Arturo caught her as she moved away and made her look into his eyes. "I've never been more serious about anything in my life, Hero. I'm in this...are you in this with me?"

She had no idea how to answer him.

BACK IN COMO, he took her back to her hotel. Kissing her goodbye, he cupped her face in his hands. "Tonight? Dinner?"

Hero hesitated. "Can I take a rain check tonight? I just have some stuff I need to figure out."

Arturo didn't seem fazed. "Of course, my darling. You have my cell phone number if you change your mind."

Hero took the stairs to her room, wanting to take her time. God, what was she going to do? She had fallen for him so entirely that even the thought of him finding out about the apartment made her feel sick. Should she put it back up for auction and take a hit on the price? She could sell it to him anonymously, maybe.

The thing was...she loved the apartment. Ever since she'd walked into it that first day—was it really only four days ago?—she had known it was her haven. Her heart was telling her that Arturo was worth giving it up; her head was telling her not to be foolish. Stick to her plan. A gorgeous man wasn't worth giving it up for.

Was he?

Shoot. Hero sighed as she opened the door to her room, then froze. Three more envelopes on the floor. She grabbed them and ran back down to the reception. She asked to see the security guard after the receptionist denied that any of her staff delivered the letters.

"Do you have CCTV?"

"I'm afraid it is currently out of order, Signorina." He looked at the envelopes in her hand curiously. "What is in the notes?"

Hero stared at him and then shook her head. "Never mind."

She stalked back upstairs, but before she locked herself in, she checked in every part of the room. She was alone. She double-locked the door and sat on the bed, the envelopes laid out in front of her. After a moment, she ripped the first one open.

Whore.

"Charming." She steeled herself for the next one.

Dead woman walking.

"Oh, fuck off." It helped a little to ridicule the note. She opened the third. There was no note, but two photographs fell out. Hero frowned, but she bent to pick them up. As she studied them, she gave a gasp of horror.

The first showed a woman: cowed, terrified, and screaming. Her dark hair was covering most of her face, but Hero could see the resemblance to herself immediately. The second photo was even more horrifying. The same woman was obviously dead, covered in blood, the hilt of a knife protruding from her stomach.

"Jesus." Hero didn't know how long she sat there, staring at the horror in front of her, but eventually, uncurling her stiff legs, she went back down to reception, feeling as if all her blood had frozen in her veins. She asked them to call the police.

When two officers arrived at the hotel, she calmly handed them the notes and simply said, "Someone wants to kill me. And I have no idea why."

CHAPTER NINE

The next morning, Hero got another message, this time phoned through to reception and of an altogether more pleasant kind. George Galiano was inviting her to have lunch with him.

Hero considered. She didn't want to get into the middle of anything between Arturo and George, but the more allies she had in this town, the better.

She called him back and agreed to meet him at the restaurant. "I can't wait," he said in a warm voice. Hero promised herself she could make it clear that it was just lunch as friends.

Until then, she had a few hours to kill, and she spent it arranging furniture for her apartment to be delivered by the end of the week. Now that it was officially hers, she was antsy to move in and be less vulnerable. She arranged for locks to be fitted to the windows, even as unlikely as it was that anyone could scale up to that height, and a deadbolt fixed to the door. It would be her little fortress. She noticed that the other apartments had just started getting renovated for individual sale, and Hero was glad that there would be plenty of construction workers around should anything happen.

God, you sound paranoid. But the vicious, utterly random threats had affected her more than she wanted to admit. The polizia had been sympathetic, but they told her there was nothing much they could do unless she were actually harmed.

"Do you know who that woman is?"

They'd studied the photographs and exchanged loaded looks, but both swore blind they didn't know who she was. "It's probably some hoax," the kindly lead officer said. "Some people just like to frighten a woman on her own."

They made it sound like she should expect this kind of thing, being on her own. Hero's feminist hackles went up, and she gathered up the notes and photos, and thanked them stiffly before turning away. She almost dared someone to attack her as she walked back through the lobby.

Come at me...

Her fear had turned to anger now, and she stalked past the hotel's security guard without acknowledging him.

George Galiano was waiting for her, sitting at one of the restaurant's outside tables, smoking a cigarette with a glass of red wine in front of him. He stood when she approached and kissed both of her cheeks. "You look beautiful, Miss Donati. Please, join me."

Over a lunch of fresh crab salad, he asked her about her plans for the apartment.

"To be honest, Mr. Galiano, I just want a haven. I've arranged for it to be furnished, of course, but beyond that, I hadn't thought."

"Well, I know some good interior designers, should you require them." He paused. "I see Bachi has already begun to remodel the other apartments."

"He owns them all, then?"

George nodded, a nasty gleam in his eyes. "As I told you, you pissed him off royally by beating him to that last one. Bachi has dreams, I think, of owning every major hotel in this region, maybe even in Italy. His plans are, like him, ridiculously conceited."

"I think it's healthy to have ambition," Haven said carefully.

George smirked. "You are very generous, Miss Donati."

"Hero, please."

"Hero. Such a pretty name. Tell me, Hero…has Arturo's legendary prowess in the bedroom been exaggerated?"

Ugh. Hero looked at him steadily. "If anything, it's been underplayed."

But George laughed. "Fair enough. I meant no offense. I only asked because I wanted to see how loyal you were to him."

"I'm as loyal as I would be to any…friend. I've been here less than a week, Mr. Galiano, I have no interest in being drawn into disputes between the two of you."

"Understood." His smile faded, and he sighed. "For my part, I wish I could understand why we drifted apart, how it got so awkward between us."

Hero's curiosity got the better of her. "You mentioned a woman you both loved before."

He nodded. "Flavia. She died twenty years ago now. She was a beautiful woman, like yourself, but that beauty was to be her downfall."

"How so?"

George's eyes were haunted. "She was murdered, stabbed to death. They never caught her killer."

The brief look on Arturo's face suddenly flashed in front of her eyes, followed by the images of the woman in the picture Hero had received earlier, and she went cold.

"Stabbed?"

George nodded. "Multiple times. She never stood a chance.

It devastated the town, myself and Arturo the most. I think neither of us has been the same since. Of course, Arturo was her lover at the time, and so the general consensus was that he was the only one suffering." He shook his head. "But I sound like a bitter man."

The realization that Arturo had also lost someone he dearly loved in some way cemented the connection between them even further. Suddenly Hero had to admit it to herself—she was falling hard for him, in more ways than between the sheets. It now seemed impossible to avoid coming clean to him about the apartment and trying to make it right.

"Mr. Galiano, thank you for lunch, but I have to go now."

George stood as she did and kissed her cheek, lingering perhaps a beat too long for her comfort. He took her hands, searching her eyes. "Please know, Hero…Arturo is not your only option. Please be careful. He is not who he says he is."

Hero pulled her hands away, her expression steely. "Thank you for the warning, Mr. Galiano."

Creep. Hero bid him goodbye and got out of there, much to her relief. *Not my only option. Ugh, the arrogance of the man.*

She felt the need to connect with someone from back home and so, as she walked to her new apartment, she called Imelda, getting only her voicemail. "Melly…I'm just touching base. Call me back. I need to hear your voice." She gave a small chuckle as she ended the call. She'd never said that to her sister…*ever.* Funny how distance changed relationships. Hero stuck her phone back into her bag and carried on towards the Patrizzi.

PETER'S FACE was blank with disappointment. "You don't like it."

He and Arturo were at an old rundown hotel on the north shore of the lake. Peter had seen it last minute and had been sure Arturo would go for it. It had an old-world rustic charm as well as a fantastic terrace overlooking the lake. A stone pergola draped in the most glorious wisteria led to lush gardens of azalea, camellia, and jasmine conveying beautiful scent along the breeze. The hotel itself had been abandoned for so long that vines had snaked their way into the interior, giving the whole place a strange but organic post-apocalyptic feel.

Peter had fallen in love with it at first sight, but he could tell from Arturo's expression that his friend felt differently. He sighed. "So, no?"

Arturo turned to him, and Peter felt a shock run through him. He'd been wrong...Arturo's eyes were shining. "It's incredible...but not for a hotel. God, Peter..."

Peter was confused. "So, let me get this right, you don't want it for a hotel, but you love it?"

"For a home, Pete. For a family home."

"A family home?" Peter echoed in confusion. "For whom?"

Arturo laughed. "For me, of course. For the family I intend to have in the future." He didn't say with whom, but Peter knew this expression of old.

"Turo...you've known her for *less than a week*." Peter stared at his old friend in astonishment. Arturo was known for being impulsive when it came to absolutely everything except relationships. In that particular area, he could always be trusted to love 'em and leave 'em. "A week," Peter repeated. "What makes her any different, Turo?"

Arturo shrugged. "You need to meet her, Peter, and then you'll understand. She's bright and funny and beautiful and I'm crazy about her."

"So crazy you're imagining your future estate together already? This isn't you," Peter said, "you're obviously having some sort of...God, I don't know, but you need to slow down."

"You don't believe in love at first sight?"

Peter rolled his eyes. "No. I don't. *At all.* Wanting to screw her isn't the same as love, Arturo. I don't need to tell you that."

"It's not that. If it were that, I'd be over it already. But she's... look, I'm going to call her and arrange for you two to meet. Then you'll see."

Peter was about to protest, but Arturo had already pulled out his phone. Peter watched the smile spread over Arturo's face as the woman answered his call.

"*Bueno giorno, bella.* How are you? Good. Listen, are you free for a drink this afternoon? I'd love you to meet my best friend, Peter Armley. Yes? Great, see you soon, *cara mia.*"

Arturo was—there really was no other word for it—*glowing* when he ended the call and smiled at Peter. "You'll see, Pete. She's perfect."

Peter held his tongue. Sometimes it paid to pull your punches with Arturo until the right moment. He usually figured things out for himself first anyway. "And what about this place?"

"I want it, but for myself. Can you get it done?"

Peter sighed, watching his hotel dreams vanish in a puff of Arturo's fantasies. "Of course, but are you sure? There's no rush with this; it's been on the market for five years without a taker. Take some time. Think about it."

Arturo shook his head. "I want it. Give the owner what he's asking for and get the paperwork through as soon as possible. I want to bring Hero here and show her what I have planned."

"*Jesus,*" Peter hissed under his breath.

It was only an hour later when they walked into a bar in Como and saw Hero Donati waiting for them that Peter understood. He took one look at the beautiful woman sitting elegantly, her long, dark hair pulled over her shoulder, her large brown eyes shining at them, and immediately saw the striking—no, not striking—the almost *uncanny* resemblance to Flavia, and he turned to Arturo, horror in his eyes.

"Arturo," he said, "what have you done?"

10

CHAPTER TEN

Hero liked Peter Armley very much, but she was a little bemused by the way he kept staring at her as if he knew her from someplace. Arturo, if he noticed it, didn't say anything, and all three of them chatted lightly.

Peter stayed until the early evening and then excused himself. "Dinner plans." He kissed Hero's cheek. "It's wonderful to meet you, Hero. Welcome to Como."

After he'd gone, she and Arturo lingered over a pre-dinner aperitif. Arturo stroked her face. "Are you hungry?"

She shook her head. To tell the truth, all Hero wanted was to be wrapped up in his arms, feeling safe and cared for. He pressed his lips to hers. "I have an idea."

"Oh?"

"There's a moonlight boat trip out on the water tonight. There will be other couples there, but I thought you might like it."

Hero smiled. "I would love that. This really is a beautiful town, Arturo."

"I'm glad you like it." He kissed her again. "Hero...I don't want to come on too strong and scare you away, but I would really like to see where this goes. You and I. Cards on the table... I haven't felt like this, perhaps ever."

Hero smiled, but the desire to ask him about Flavia was in the forefront of her mind. She had to be the girl in the pictures she had been sent, and even Hero could see the likeness between them. Knowing Arturo had loved the dead girl, and now someone was threatening Hero's own life...could she trust him?

Was Arturo the man behind the threats? Hero knew she should end this thing between them and yet she couldn't. "What time is the boat trip?"

"Nine." Arturo's green eyes were intense on hers. "We have a few hours to kill."

Hero felt his fingers stroke the inside of her thigh and she moaned softly. God, why did he have this effect on her? He was addictive. She nuzzled his ear and whispered, "Arturo. Take me home and fuck me into next week..."

Arturo grinned widely, and in twenty minutes, he was stripping her dress from her body as they kissed, clawing at each other. "Don't wait." Hero gasped, and Arturo thrust his cock deep into her cunt, fucking her furiously until they both fell from the bed, laughing and teasing each other. Arturo gathered her to him and slid back into her, and their lovemaking slowed. They took their time, building the intensity between them until Hero came, her back arching up, her belly against his, her head thrown back as she cried out.

"God, you're intoxicating," Arturo groaned as he came, then they collapsed together, panting for air. "Hero...*il mia amore*..."

There was such tenderness in his voice that Hero kissed him and rolled on top of him. "I want to taste you."

He grinned up at her. "Darling, I would like nothing more. Just let me deal with this condom."

As he used the bathroom, Hero waited, stretched out luxuriously on the bed. Every time she was naked with him, she felt so...what was the word...? Sensual, feminine...he made her feel beautiful. As he came back into the room, his magnificent cock already half-erect again, she gazed at him, blatant lust in her eyes. He approached the bed, and she sat up, taking his cock into her mouth, running her tongue along the length of it, feeling the hardening muscle under the silky skin. Arturo groaned as she began to suck, tease, and draw on the sensitive tip, her fingernails digging into his buttocks.

As he came, shooting thick creamy cum onto her tongue, she swallowed it down and then smiled up at him. Arturo pushed her back on the bed, and hitched her legs around his waist, kissing her passionately. "You drive me crazy, Hero."

His cock nudged at the entrance of her cunt then buried itself deep inside her. Arturo's lovemaking was almost frenzied now, his domination over her body complete, and Hero came again and again as he fucked her, his cock pounding at her until he, too, came.

As they recovered, Hero groaned. "We did it again. Shoot."

"What?"

She sighed. "Forgot the damn condom. *Jesus.*"

He stroked her back as she sat up. "*Cara mia*, you do not have to worry. I have a clean medical record as far as STDs go. If you don't believe me, I can have you call my physician for confirmation."

Hero relaxed a little. "It's not just that, though. There's pregnancy to consider too."

Arturo sat up and kissed her shoulder. "Would that be the worst thing?"

She gaped at him. "A week, Arturo. A *week*. No, don't." She wriggled away as he tried to wrap his arms around her. "This is all too much." Hero rolled out of bed and shook her head. "First, you mention marriage and now this? Slow the hell *down*."

She ran her hand through her hair, pacing up and down. Arturo watched her. "I'm sorry, Hero. I get a little overexcited sometimes, and I guess...I'm spoilt. I'm used to getting what I want when I want it, and sometimes I forget about other people's feelings. I'm sorry."

Hero was taken aback by his honesty and her panic, so overwhelming just a moment ago, faded. *Talk to him.* She sat back down on the bed. "Arturo...I'm just not ready for something so serious, so...final. There's a lot going on in my life and, well...I just got here. That's not to say I don't love being with you. I do, I really do, but we need to slow down. Please."

"Of course. I really am sorry." He sighed, but gave her space, not reaching for her again immediately. "I never thought I could feel like this again."

"After...Flavia?" Hero said quietly.

A long silence. "Yes. So, you also Googled me, I take it?"

Here we go.

"No." She looked at him. "I had lunch with George Galiano today."

She watched his expression go from shock to anger to jealousy to acceptance. "I see."

"Just as...acquaintances. We met at the auction." So, a little lie, but it didn't matter. "He was kind enough to tell me all about your beef with him."

Arturo snorted. "I bet he did."

Hero half-grinned at him. "You don't have to worry...he's kind of a creep."

"You're not wrong." Arturo laughed, looking relieved. "So... he told you about Flavia?"

She nodded. "Arturo, I'm so very sorry. Why didn't you say anything? Especially after I told you about Tom and Beth."

"I didn't want to freak you out," he admitted.

"Because we look alike?"

Arturo nodded. "You do. When I saw you that first time, I thought I'd seen her ghost. But, Hero, listen. You are two totally different people, and I know that. Your resemblance to Flavia is incidental to how I feel about you, I swear. I *swear*."

She nodded but wanted more than that. "What kind of woman was she?"

"First of all, let me say this. You are a woman. Flavia was a girl. She was eighteen when she was murdered. And she...I loved her, I truly loved her, and she loved me. But she also loved men and loved sex, and after her death, I found out she had been sleeping with George, too. He was my friend at the time, and I believe he enjoyed telling me that my sainted girlfriend had been a cheater. As you can imagine...we've rarely spoken since."

"What an asshole," Hero shook her head. "What a spiteful, needless thing to do." She put her hand on his face. "You're a million times the man he is, Turo."

Arturo smiled. "I like that. You calling me Turo." He leaned in slowly, and she met him halfway, giving permission for the soft kiss, but then his smile faded. "They never caught the killer, and I never found out why she died. Maybe it was another jealous lover? I don't know. The polizia found nothing." He shook his head. "I still have nightmares about her end...her terrible fear and pain."

Hero felt sick. *Tell him. Tell him about the notes, the threats...* but she couldn't do it. Couldn't give him that kind of worry again. She kissed him softly. "I'm so sorry, Turo."

Arturo wrapped his arms around her. "You make it better, *cara mia*."

She leaned into him and sighed. "I hope I do. You make my pain go away, Turo. I hope, one day, I could do the same for you."

"You already have."

They made love again, and this time, it wasn't the frenzied

fucking of before; it was something more, the forging of a deeper connection, their gazes never parting.

At nine o'clock, Arturo took her on the boat trip around the lake, and they snuggled down in their seats, enjoying the night, laughing together, hands clasped. It was the perfect end to an intense day, and Hero felt herself relaxing with this man. She still had to tell him about the apartment, but she had decided if he really wanted it...she didn't want to lose him over it. They could work something out.

From the other end of the boat, he watched them. There was something different about the way they were together now: a new understanding, a new closeness.

Perfect.

He wondered if Hero Donati would scream when he drove his knife into her over and over and over again...

CHAPTER ELEVEN

Hero packed the last of her things into her bag and threw it over her shoulder. She glanced around the hotel room which had been her home for the last ten days and felt nervous. Today, she would move into the Patrizzi apartment, and later, she would tell Arturo what she had done. She couldn't justify spending any more money on hotel rooms now. She had a five-million-euro apartment, and she had to live there.

The cab took her to the apartment, and she opened the door and stepped into her new home. It echoed with silence, but with the furniture in place, it had the beginnings of a real home.

She pushed open the doors to the small balcony and stepped out into the air, breathing in great lungfuls of air. *Home.* She couldn't help the small thrill that ran through her, but it was tempered with sadness. Tonight, she would tell Arturo, and it would either be the end of them…or the beginning of something else.

Her cell phone rang.

"*Finally.*" Hero said as her sister said hello.

"Don't be a pain, my phone got dropped in the bath."

"You mean *you* dropped it in the bath."

She grinned as Imelda sighed. "Fine. How are you?"

"Good. I moved into the apartment."

"Good. That's good. Is everything else okay? You sounded... weird on the voicemail you left."

Hero hesitated. "I'm fine. I just wanted to touch base. How're Mom and Dad?" A spike of adrenaline ran through her when her sister hesitated. "Melly?"

Imelda sighed. "Don't panic...but Pops had a little heart thing. He's okay, he's fine, but..."

"Oh God, Melly." Hero walked back inside and dropped onto the couch, her heart racing, her insides frozen. "I'll get on a plane. I'll book a flight this second and—"

"No, you will not. I said don't panic. He's going to be okay; they're just keeping him in for observation. He's fine, sis. Honestly. It was just a little bit of a scare."

That lessened Hero's panic only marginally. "How could you not tell me?"

"Because Mom said not to. Because she says—and I agree—you need this. You need to be away from Chicago, making your own life. Dad is fine, I promise, and I will absolutely call you if anything changes. But you stay there, Hero. You need to do this."

Hero was silent for a long time. "You promise you'll tell me if he gets worse?"

"I promise." Imelda let out a long breath, and when she spoke again, her voice was softer. "Hero...are you doing okay?"

Hero choked back a sob and steadied her voice. "I'm fine. It's beautiful here."

"Made friends?"

More than that... "A couple."

"Good. Sweetheart, you did the right thing. I'm proud of you."

Hero was too shocked to reply, and she heard Imelda's soft

laugh. "Take care, little sister. And believe me, I do actually care. I'll see you soon."

The phone clicked off before Hero could reply. She sat for a moment, trying to take in her sister's words. First, the news about her dad, and then just now...that had been the closest to 'I love you' she'd ever gotten from Imelda.

The world is shifting on its axis.

Hero shook her head and before she could change her mind, she called Arturo and got his voicemail.

ARTURO CHECKED his voicemail an hour later as he sat in his office and frowned. "That was weird."

Peter looked up at him, putting down the sheaf of papers he held. "What?"

"That was Hero. She wants to meet later...at the Patrizzi apartment."

Peter frowned. "Why on earth?"

"I have no idea." Arturo tried calling her back. "Hey, it's me. Look, of course I can meet you there, but what's going on, Hero? Well, call me back if you can, but I'll be there at six."

He ended the call and put his phone down on the desk, chewing his bottom lip. "That's very strange."

Peter half-smiled. "Maybe Hero's the buyer?"

Arturo rolled his eyes. "Yeah, because she has millions of euros just laying around."

"She might."

Arturo looked at Peter over his glasses. "Really? You think so?"

"No. Listen, can we get back to this? Villa Claudia is yours as soon as you sign. I can't believe you got it for a half-million."

Arturo grinned. "By the time I've finished with it, it'll be worth ten times that. Not that I'll be selling."

"Still planning your marital home with the lovely Hero?"

"What's your problem?" Arturo looked up at the cynical tone in Peter's voice, his eyes narrowing. "Don't you like Hero?"

"I liked her very, very much, Turo. She's sweet and smart and beautiful." Peter fixed him with a hard look. "And she looks just like your murdered girlfriend. *Jesus*, Arturo, just how fucked up are you?"

Arturo sat back and sighed. "She's a completely different person, Pete."

"How?"

"She's Hero and not Flavia, for one," he said dryly and rolled his eyes at Peter's look. "She's also American, you know. Versus Italian. Big difference there. And she's softer somehow, yet at the same time, more assured. Wiser. She's a woman. Flavia…" Arturo felt the usual sadness at the memory of such a beautiful young life cut short. "Flavia was just a kid. Hero was married, you know, with a child."

Pete's eyebrows shot up. "*Was?*"

"They died in a car wreck two years ago."

"Jesus. How old is Hero?"

"Twenty-eight."

Peter shook his head. "Fuck. She tell you about them?"

"Yup." Arturo leaned forward. "And I told her about Flavia, including the fact that they resemble each other. Sadly, I didn't get there first. George told Hero about Flavia."

"She knows *George*?" Peter looked bemused.

Arturo chuckled.

"Yup. She thinks he's a creep."

"She gets points for judging that character right, at least."

Arturo smirked. "Anyway, he took her to lunch, tried to pull his usual con job, but she saw straight through him. But, yeah, he told her about Flavia."

"And she wasn't scared off?"

Arturo didn't hide his smile. "Nope. But she did tell me to slow down."

"Good." Peter sighed. "More points in her favor."

Arturo nodded, his face becoming serious. "Pete...she's special. I know you think it's because of Flav, but it really isn't. She's...very dear to me. Yes. Already."

Peter studied his best friend. "You're in love with her."

"Yes."

"Does she know?"

Arturo took a deep breath in. "I haven't said it. The whole 'slow down' thing, you see. But yes, I'm in love with Hero Donati."

And he could see that, finally, Peter believed him.

AT SIX P.M., Arturo drove into town and parked outside the Patrizzi. He spoke to some of his contractors, noting the work already done, then headed up to the apartment. It was quiet on the top floor, and he strode around the corridors. The apartment was in the farthest corner away from the elevators, and as he approached, he could see the door was open. He frowned. Why the hell was Hero here?

He stepped into the apartment and then recoiled in shock at all the blood. At the body. "Oh God, no...no...NO!"

CHAPTER TWELVE

"Hero? Miss Donati? Can you hear me? If you can, please open your eyes or squeeze my hand."

Nothing. The paramedic looked at his partner. "She's really out."

Arturo gritted his teeth, holding back a scream of frustration. From the moment he'd walked in and found her passed out on the floor, he had cradled Hero in his arms as he waited for the emergency services, and he'd called her name over and over, but she'd refused to wake. His clothes were drenched in her blood, paramedics were all over the place, and *still* she refused to wake.

And now he couldn't hold her, because she was being prodded by half a dozen medics. All he could do was clench his teeth in frustration and try to thank God that at least she was alive. Or so they kept telling him.

"She has a nasty gash on her scalp. Scalp wounds always bleed like a mother...I'd say she was hit from behind, or maybe she fell against something. Yes, there. Look..." The paramedic pointed to the metal range in the kitchen. "She could have fallen or been pushed—the police will find out."

Arturo couldn't take his eyes off Hero, so pale, her golden skin so yellow and wan. "Will she be okay?"

"We need to get her checked out."

He rode in the ambulance with them, holding Hero's hand. As they neared the hospital, she groaned and opened her eyes. "Turo?"

Relief rushed through him so powerfully that if he'd been standing, he would've gone weak-kneed. "Hero, thank God...I'm here, *bella*. I'm right here, sweetheart."

Her dark eyes swam with tears, and Arturo was about to call out to a medic that she was in pain when her voice stopped him.

"I'm so sorry."

Arturo frowned. "*Cara mia*, why are you apologizing? Whatever happened, it was in no way your fault."

The ambulance stopped, and then they were taking her through to the emergency room. Arturo held her hand gently as she looked at him, pain in her eyes.

"I'm so sorry, baby," she said again, her voice weakening, "it was me. *I* was the one who bought the Patrizzi apartment..."

Arturo let go of her hand as the nursing staff stopped him at the door, staring after her, not understanding for a moment what she had told him. They took Hero through the doors to the ICU, and he lost sight of her.

Shocked to his core by her admission, and by the horror of her accident—or attack—Arturo didn't think. He turned on his heel and walked out of the hospital.

Fliss Seymour jumped into the hospital room with a flourish. "Ta-da!"

Hero, despite her pounding head and the heavy weight that

had settled on her chest, chuckled. "You loon. Thank you for coming, Fliss...I didn't know who else to call." *And the man I'm crazy about hates me now...*

Fliss hugged her gingerly. "It's my pleasure, love. Are you okay?"

"Just a concussion and some wounded pride."

Fliss peered at her. "And some pretty radical bruises. You got all that from falling over?"

No.

"My own fault. I tripped over some shoes I left lying around." *As the man who was trying to kill me beat my head against the metal range.* She closed her eyes for a moment.

"You okay? Should I get a nurse?"

Hero opened her eyes. "No, just some dizziness. Fliss, really, thank you."

Fliss grinned at her. "I was going to bring flowers, but I thought you'd enjoy these more." She brought out a small box and handed it to Hero. Inside was a row of chunky, jewel-colored soft pastels.

Hero grinned. "These are beautiful, but you have to let me pay for them."

"No way...but, you could share some gossip I heard."

"What's that?" Hero was admiring the deep, rich red of one of the pastels. Fliss grinned.

"Word is...Arturo Bachi was the one who brought you in, and he was pretty upset."

Hero's heart sank. "He was the one who found me."

"Because *you* were the one who bought the Patrizzi apartment!" Fliss crowed, obviously enjoying herself. "Man, I bet the polizia went to town on him."

Hero frowned. "The police?"

"They arrested him on suspicion of attacking you."

"No, no, no, it wasn't him, *it wasn't him*...oh my God, no!" Hero felt hysteria bubbling up inside her.

Fliss looked alarmed and got up to hug her. "Ssh, ssh, it's okay. Calm down. They let him go. He had more than one alibi. But, Hero...so someone did attack you?"

Hero nodded. "Yes. But it wasn't Arturo. I *swear* it wasn't."

"I believe you." Fliss's usually merry face was somber. "Are you planning on telling the polizia."

Hero nodded. "Yes. I just...I have to get my mind around things first." How do you get your mind around almost having your head bashed in?

"Okay. And you and Bachi...?"

"Not anymore," Hero whispered, still aching at the fact that he wasn't by her side. That he had left when she needed him so badly. "Not anymore. Not after..." The weight on her chest grew too heavy then, and she began to sob quietly.

"Oh, sweetheart." Fliss wrapped her arms around her and held her as she cried herself out. Finally, Fliss swept Hero's damp hair away from her forehead. "Listen, when are they letting you out?"

"A couple of days."

"Well, then, you can stay with me. For as long as you need. I have a guest bedroom; it's warm and safe. No arguments."

Hero smiled at her. "Anyone tell you you're the best?"

"Frequently." Fliss grinned. "Now, I think you should get some sleep, sweetheart. Do you need some sleeping pills?"

Hero shook her head. "But I could do with some pain killers."

Fliss squeezed her hand. "Be right back, babe."

Later, alone, Hero fell into a fitful sleep, tormented by images of Arturo's beautiful face full of rage and hatred for her. She didn't understand him walking away so coldly—it was only an apartment, and he'd said he had real feelings for her. Even so, she should have told him sooner. She didn't care about the damn apartment now. He could have it.

But the thought of him being in the world and hating her made her miserable. Even in this short time, she knew...she loved Arturo Bachi. And now she would have to live through the heartbreak of knowing she would never see him again.

CHAPTER THIRTEEN

"Run that past me again. *Hero* bought the Patrizzi apartment?"

Arturo gave a quick nod. Peter sat back in his chair, clearly stunned. "And someone attacked her there?"

"So it seems. But who?"

"Does she have any idea?"

Arturo looked away from Peter's intense gaze and said nothing. Peter sighed. "You haven't been to see her."

"No."

"You mad?"

"Yes. And no. Hell, I don't know what to think. She kept it from me all that time."

Peter fixed him with a glare. "*All that time*? Arturo, it's been less than two weeks. Maybe she didn't know how to tell you. Maybe she got scared. Maybe she didn't want you to find out."

"Then why did she invite me to the apartment? She knew." Arturo got up and stared out of the window.

Peter watched him.

"Turo," he said in a soft voice, "I told you not to fall in love with her."

"Doesn't matter. It's over now."

"Forgive her. It's just a damn apartment. Damn it, Turo. You claim to love her, but you don't have a clue what love is if you're holding something so petty over the woman's bashed-in head!"

Arturo turned and gave him a sad smile. "I forgave her the second she told me. It's a matter of her forgiving me, and I don't think that's going to happen. I walked away, Pete. I walked away when she needed me the most. How the hell can I ask for forgiveness for that?"

The look on Pete's face told him his friend more than agreed.

ARTURO OPENED the envelope and drew out the documents, frowning. What the hell? It was the deed to the Patrizzi apartment. In *his* name. What the fuck?

"Marcie? Who dropped these papers off?"

Marcella came in. "Young girl. Short, curly hair. English. Very sweet. What are they?"

Arturo handed her the documents, and she read them, her eyes widening. "Wow. So, you finally bought the apartment?"

"No. That's why I'm confused."

The phone at Marcie's desk buzzed, and she went back out, closing the door behind her.

Arturo read through the paperwork again. So, Hero was giving him the apartment? No, no way, this must be a mistake. But there it was in black and white. His dream, handed to him on a plate and it hadn't cost him a penny.

It just cost him the woman he loved. The real dream.

FLISS INSISTED on taking care of everything, having Hero's things moved from the apartment—the apartment where she'd never even spent *one* night—to Fliss's large and beautifully furnished guest room.

"I'm paying rent," Hero insisted, and although Fliss rolled her eyes, Hero wouldn't take no for an answer.

She and the English woman became close very quickly, and as the weeks passed, Hero even began to help out in the little art store. One day, she was alone in the store when a man she didn't recognize came in, smartly dressed. "Miss Donati?"

Her guard went up immediately. "Who's asking?"

He had a kind smile. "I work for Signore Bachi. He asked me to bring you this." He handed her an envelope, nodded, and left the store.

Hero stared at the envelope. Hearing Arturo's name left her simultaneously hot and cold inside. God...she both wanted to know what he said and was terrified at the same time. She braced herself and tore it open.

There was no note, just a check in the amount of five million Euros. The message was clear. Arturo didn't want any more ties to her.

"Oh, damn it, damn it," Hero murmured, tears pooling in her eyes. There went the last hope. She stuffed the check back in the envelope and then raised it to her face. She could smell his fresh, spicy scent on the envelope, and a memory came rushing back of his skin next to hers, his lips on hers hungry for her kisses, his arms around her. The way he would brace his arms either side of her head as his cock thrust deep into her, driving her towards ecstasy. The love in his eyes.

Hero dropped her head and began to cry. *Pull yourself together.* But she couldn't. It was a different kind of loss, a fresh one, and the pain was overwhelming.

From his hidden position outside across the piazza, he watched her. Arturo's chest hurt as he saw her weeping. Was it from relief that he'd paid for the apartment? Or was it pain over their parting?

He had lost any anger he felt towards her for the apartment. Hell, he'd lost any passion he'd had for anything now. Arturo knew he could walk over to the shop to see her and beg for her forgiveness...but the thought that she might send him away? His courage failed him. His heart simply would not stand it. He knew now that he'd loved Flavia like the selfish boy that he'd been—he loved Hero like the man she'd tempted him to truly be.

Arturo turned away and walked quickly to the police station. He might not be with Hero any longer, but he was damned if he'd stop trying to find out who attacked her. The police had questioned him, yes, but he still had influence.

He found out more when he asked to talk to the lead detective. "Signorina Donati was getting threats, Signore Bachi. Death threats. She came to us last week with some of the notes, but there was nothing we could do. That's all I can tell you."

Arturo just managed to keep his temper; blowing up wouldn't get him any more information. "But someone did attack her? Are you giving her protection?"

"We don't have the manpower."

Arturo was steaming angry when he left the station. Getting on the phone, he asked his security chief to arrange protection for Hero. "But—and this is important—she mustn't know. They must be discreet, and I don't want her spied on." He outlined what else he needed and ended the call. He was so tempted to go back to the little side street with the quaint little art store but stopped himself. It would just cause him more pain. Worse yet, it would just hurt her more, and that he could not justify, no matter how much he ached.

Instead, he drove to the office and went to find Peter, who took one look at him and grabbed his jacket. "Come on."

"Where are we going?"

"The *Villa Claudia*. You need something to distract you."

HERO WAS LOCKING the shop when she heard her name being called. Turning, she saw a smiling George Galiano walking towards her, and her heart sank. Arranging her features into a smile, she greeted him.

"*Ciao, bella*." He kissed her on the cheek, then nodded to the store. "You work here now?"

"Just helping out."

He nodded. "I see. I was just passing, and I thought it was you. Come, have a drink with me."

Out of politeness, Hero went with him to a bar out on the lakefront.

"Shall we sit outside? It's such a warm evening."

Hero didn't care. "Fine."

George chatted pleasantly for a while about nothing in particular, and Hero barely listened to him. Then he sat back and studied her. "I heard some things. Your accident? I'm very sorry. Are you still in pain?"

"No." Not physically.

"And you and Arturo? I heard you split."

Hero sighed. "For something that was private, news sure travels fast."

"This is a small town, Hero, and Arturo, for some reason, is always a source of gossip and chatter."

"You seem to take an interest."

George shrugged. "Arturo and I...we go back a long way."

"You told me. Flavia cheated on him with you." It came out

as an accusation, and Hero regretted it the moment it left her mouth.

George leaned forward, and his eyes gleamed with malice. "She did. She was desperately unhappy with Arturo, but I don't suppose he mentioned that. He always likes to paint himself as the innocent one in all of this. He'll do it to you, too; make out that you're the villain, the gold-digger who used him and then dumped him."

Hero recoiled from his spite. "That isn't the man I know."

"You've known him two weeks, Hero." George sat back. "I've known him a lifetime."

"Look, I think I'd better go." Hero got to her feet. "I really don't want to get involved in any conflict between you and Arturo."

George laughed. "You don't get it, do you? You are already involved. You were involved the moment you fucked Arturo."

Furious, Hero turned away from him...and ran straight into Arturo.

14

CHAPTER FOURTEEN

Arturo stared at her and felt a desperate longing to take her in his arms and kiss the pain out of her eyes. Hero looked pale, angry, and achingly beautiful. "Hero..."

Her eyes filled with tears. "Hello, Turo."

God, when she said his name like that...

"Look, I..."

Then he saw him: George Galiano, getting to his feet. Arturo's heart froze and his jaw set. "Galiano."

Hero—*God*, she was so beautiful—looked down at her feet, her face reddening, and Galiano looked smug. What the hell was she doing with *him*?

George looked triumphant, his eyes shining with malevolence. "Bachi. Armley," he added to Peter, who was standing behind Arturo. Arturo cut his eyes back to Hero, who looked up and met his gaze.

No one said anything for a long moment, tension crackling in the air between them. Abruptly, Hero, her hand at her mouth, stepped away from all three of them, ran across the piazza, and disappeared into a side street.

Arturo stared after her, his heart breaking. *Come back. Come back, I love you, I'm sorry...*

"You were careless with that little girl's heart. Just like you were with Flavia's." George Galiano's voice seared into his brain, and Arturo turned back to him, fists clenching.

"You leave her alone, Galiano. Hero Donati is not a game you can use to win points from me."

George laughed. "I'm not playing any sort of game, Arturo. I'm just stating a fact. And besides, you probably gave up any right to her heart by dumping her at the hospital. What kind of man does that?"

Arturo didn't reply because he was too busy punching George from across the table. George slammed backwards into three more, tipping them over, causing patrons of the café to jump to their feet.

PETE PRACTICALLY THREW Arturo into his car, and he drove away before Arturo could get out and pound on George some more. "Jesus, Turo." He shook his head as they sped out of town and towards Arturo's home. "You have got to get your head on straight again."

Arturo, his anger dissipating slumped in the driver's seat. "Did you see her? God, she looked so hurt."

Peter sighed. "Turo, you're not going to like what I have to say...but you two together...it's toxic. You're bad for each other. Stay away from her."

ARTURO WANTED TO ARGUE, but he had no strength left. His misery was consuming him. After Pete finally extracted a promise from him later that evening that he wouldn't seek her out, he was left alone. Arturo couldn't stop thinking about her though: the still-vivid bruises on her face, the sorrow in her eyes. He knew she loved him—knew it—but maybe Peter was right. Maybe they *were* a disaster together. Maybe she wouldn't have gotten hurt, or threatened, if she'd had nothing to do with him.

He leaned his head on the cool glass of his villa window and looked out at the lights of the town. "I'm sorry," he whispered and closed his eyes.

THE NEXT MORNING, Hero awoke to raised voices. Blinking in the pale morning light, she pulled her robe on and went to find out what was going on. Fliss met her in the hallway. "You have a visitor. I told her you were asleep, but she told me to wake you up."

"She?" But then the door opened, and Hero saw her. "Melly?"

"Who else?"

Hero jumped out of bed and tackled her startled sister in a fierce hug.

FLISS, apparently terrified of Imelda, made her excuses and went to work. "Help yourself to anything you need," she told them, then said in an undertone to Hero, "Valium, heroin, morphine..."

Hero hid a smile. "Thanks, Fliss. I'm sorry if it seems I'm taking over your whole life."

"Hey, *mi casa es su casa*. I'll see you later."

Hero sucked in a deep breath and went to face her sister. Imelda was making coffee, opening the fridge and searching out some cream. She stopped when Hero came in and leaned against the doorjamb.

"So," Imelda stuck her hand on her hip and fixed Hero with

a laser beam stare, "who did *that* to you?" She stabbed a finger at the fading bruises. "Why didn't you call me when you were in the goddamn hospital...and who is this billionaire you've been fucking?"

ARTURO WALKED through the Villa Claudia trying to focus on what he wanted to do with it. The worst of it was...he had seen his future here, and it was with Hero. He could imagine her: trailing her fingers through the wisteria and the jasmine; the scent on her skin later as they danced under moonlight; candles guttering on the long stone table; the remnants of their supper; empty bottles of wine; Hero, barefoot, in a light cotton dress, her hair streaming down her back; in his arms, her lips against his.

Arturo closed his eyes and dreamed the rest of it.

Kissing her eyelids, her dark lashes sweeping down on her cheeks. Her whisper of "I love you." His fingers sliding the thin straps of her dress down her arms, the dress slipping to the ground. Her breasts, so full, so soft in his hands, the nipples hardening as his tongue swept over them. Laying her back on the thick grass of the lawn, burying his face in her sex as she writhed and gasped under him. Sucking on her clit until she was begging for him and sliding his ramrod hard cock into her softness. The flush in her cheeks when she came.

Arturo groaned and sat down on the cold stone floor. How had this happened to him? He didn't get hung up on a woman; he fucked around and never called them back. He never *ever* got involved. And he certainly never felt like this after knowing a woman for two weeks.

Fuck this shit. He would make this place into the home he imagined anyway. He would live here alone and never, ever let any woman affect him like this again.

No. No. That wouldn't work for me. For us.

Damn it.

He raised his head and looked around once more at the space, hearing Hero's soft laughter echoing through it. That did it.

I'm going to get her back.

CHAPTER FIFTEEN

"So, who did you piss off?" Imelda looked down at the notes Hero showed her and the photographs of the murdered girl.

Hero shook her head. "I don't know. I got the first one just a few days after I got here. The other three later." She thought back. "The first one...I'd just got back to the hotel, and someone had followed me. A man. He had a knife, I think."

Imelda gaped at her. "And you didn't go to the police after that?"

"No. I ignored it. Who would threaten me like that? I figured they...got the wrong room." Her excuse sounded flimsy even to her as she saw Imelda look skeptical.

"You were with *him* that night, yes?"

"Yes."

"So, you had 'fuck-brain.'"

Hero snorted with laughter. "I had *what*?"

"Fuck-brain. All those endorphins flowing through your system. You were dick-ma-tized."

Hero chuckled, feeling lighter now her sister was here. "I don't know what makes me say this, Melly, but I missed you."

Imelda studied her younger sister. "You know what's strange? I missed you, too."

"Thanks," Hero said dryly, but Imelda waved her hand.

"No, I mean...for once, when you weren't there, it was odd. And it wasn't like when you married and lived all that way down in Chicago. It felt like...you were gone. *Gone*, gone. When we didn't know where you were, I honestly thought you'd done something stupid. Hero, when I told you to move, I was just trying to shock you into doing something. I didn't actually want you to move to another country."

"I know that, Melly."

Imelda gave a little sigh. "I wasn't very nice to you when we were growing up."

"No."

"I was jealous."

Hero's eyes widened. "*You* were jealous of *me*? Why?"

"Because you were nice, and I didn't know how to be like that. I was just born a bitch."

"You are *not* a bitch," Hero said, emphatically. "You tell it how it is." She considered, then grinned. "Sometimes you might...take a scoop from the asshole jar."

They both laughed.

"God, Melly, it feels so good to laugh." Hero rubbed her face, her smile fading. "I messed up right from the beginning here."

Imelda didn't say anything for a moment, and when she spoke again, her voice was soft, kind. "Was he special?"

Hero nodded. "I've never met anyone like him, Melly, not even Tom, and God, I loved Tom. He was absolutely my best friend in the world, but Arturo..." She flushed. "I've never known...sex...like that. And the connection...God, Melly." She could feel tears threatening again. "It just felt right, you know?"

Imelda sighed and took her sister's hand. "Hero...I hate to say this because I can't forgive him for leaving you at the hospital, but if you really feel that deeply about him, maybe there's a chance?"

"I really want to believe that, but I don't think there's much hope."

Arturo finished speaking to his Board after securing their agreement to change the name of the Villa Patrizzi. He saw they didn't really care what he called it; they were just delighted that he'd acquired the last apartment, and as far as they were concerned, it was free of charge. He didn't tell them that he'd paid Hero back everything she'd paid. The cost was nothing with all his millions. Peter had been annoyed but eventually let it go. "Hey, it's your money, buddy."

Arturo grinned. "So very passive-aggressive."

Peter had laughed. "Fair enough. Listen, Philipo came out of his belfry to ask if you would go see him soon."

Arturo's uncle, Philipo, might run the Bachi Foundation, but he was a reclusive figure. Arturo could count on one hand the times he had seen his uncle in the last ten years. Peter saw his uncle more than he did, given that he was the liaison between Arturo and the trust fund his uncle handled.

Arturo was surprised now that he had been summoned, and when he and Peter drove over to see him, he was shocked to see his uncle so frail. He shot a look at Peter, who looked equally surprised.

"Uncle...how are you?"

Philipo waved his hand. "Old, my boy, so you can take that look off your face. I asked you to come here for one reason. Your fortieth birthday is a year away, but I have made the decision to release your trust fund early. There is a good chance I won't make it to your birthday. Cancer."

Arturo hadn't even begun to process that news before Philipo continued.

"No, don't look like that, I've had a good life." He looked at Peter. "But there's a caveat. Peter will now be the executor. I've not forgotten what drove your father to craft these conditions, the way you behaved."

"Uncle...my trust is the least of my concerns right now," Arturo replied. "There must be something we can do. I could take you to Sloan-Kettering to get some treatment."

Philipo shook his head. "I'm not fighting this. I'm prepared for my death, Arturo. I just want to be with my Giovanna."

The wistful look on the cranky old man's face brought Hero flooding straight back into Arturo's mind, and Philipo seemed to see right through him.

"Speaking of love..." A smile cracked the old man's visage. "I hear you have a new amore. An American girl."

Arturo cleared his throat, awkwardly, still trying to figure out how they could be discussing his love life after his uncle announced he was dying. "It's...complicated, uncle."

"Pah," his uncle spat. "Uncomplicate it, if you love her. Do you love her?"

"Very much." Arturo could sense Peter looking at him and shot him a look. "I'm going to try, uncle. Do I have your blessing?"

"What do I care? Yes, yes, have my blessing. Don't waste love, Arturo." Philipo fixed him with a stern, powerful look that had lost no ground to the disease that was killing him. "That also means don't waste time, by the way."

IN THE CAR on the way back to the office, Peter studied his friend. "You're going to try and get Hero back?"

"Yes. She's all I want, Peter. All I want. Nothing means anything without her."

Peter was silent, and Arturo knew his friend was concerned. He shot him a half-smile. "Pete, I know what you're thinking, but I'm older now. I know what I want."

"I just don't want you putting your life in the hands of someone you met two weeks ago, no matter how great she is in the sack."

Arturo sighed. "Pete, it's not just the sex with Hero...it's her. I've never had this connection with anyone...not even Flavia. You know me, I don't get involved, and yet when I met Hero, my world shifted. I realized what is important."

"But you left her at the hospital."

He winced. "Shock. Confusion. My dumbass male pride. I don't give a fuck now. I want her back. I know I always get what I want, but I think she wants it, too, Peter. We're good for each other. We're right. I need her so much...I believe she also needs me."

Peter said no more.

When Arturo got back to the office, he greeted Marcella and then went into his office and closed the door. Drawing in a lungful of air, he picked up his phone and flicked through his contacts to Hero's number and pressed 'Call.' When he heard her gentle voice, nervous and shaking, he smiled. "It's me. Can we talk?"

16

CHAPTER SIXTEEN

Arturo saw the tall, willowy blonde cross the restaurant, and was surprised when she stopped at his table. Her face, patrician and elegant, was beautiful, but her eyes were suspicious and unfriendly. "Signore Bachi?"

"That's me."

She held out her hand. "Imelda Donati."

Hero's sister. Arturo stood and shook her hand, frowning. "Is Hero okay? I'd heard she was recovering from her injuries—"

"She's fine. She's currently at home, sulking because I wouldn't let her come. May I sit?"

"Of course." He held out her chair for her, so many questions whirling around his mind. Had Hero changed her mind about seeing him? What did this woman mean by not letting Hero come?

Imelda Donati was studying him. "I can see what you're thinking. She's a twenty-eight-year-old woman. How do I get to keep her from doing whatever she wants? Signore Bachi...I wanted to see you first, to meet you, to see the man who got my sister into this mess she's in."

Arturo nodded. "In that case, let me waste none of your time.

You're here to see if I'm good enough for Hero. Let me set you straight. I'm not. I'm not good enough for her. But I'm going to do everything I can to become that man."

Imelda raised a perfectly manicured eyebrow. "You should know, Signore Bachi, that I'm not easily swayed by a pretty face, even one as handsome as yours. It'll take more than words to persuade me that you care for my sister. We nearly lost her when Tom and Beth died. When she woke after three months in a come to find her husband and daughter were dead, and I had to be the one to tell her that we buried them without her...I never want her to go through that again."

"I swear to God, I will make sure she is cared for the rest of her life if she lets me," Arturo said fiercely. "I don't want to dictate what Hero does; I want her to be free, happy, and more than anything, safe."

"Safe." Imelda's expression changed then, losing some of its blank ferociousness to fear. "Signore Bachi..."

"Please call me Arturo."

"Arturo...did you know Hero was threatened before she was attacked?"

He nodded. "I just heard recently about some notes she got before the acci...attack. She's confirmed it, then? She *was* attacked at the Villa Patrizzi?"

Imelda sighed. "Yes. A man grabbed her from behind, beat her and told her he wasn't going to kill her 'this time.'"

Arturo's mouth turned to sand, but Imelda was still talking so he couldn't lose himself in the horror or misery.

"She has no idea who he was or why he would target her. Arturo, if you care for her as much as you say you do, prove it. Help me find who is threatening my sister."

"Anything." Arturo reached across and grasped her hand, pressing firmly. "*Anything.*"

Imelda considered him, lightly turning her hand free. "Then

perhaps you can tell me who this woman is in these photographs that Hero was sent?"

She placed the two photographs on the table in front of him. Arturo's chest hurt when he stared down at them. Flavia. Hurt and terrified, then butchered. Looking so much like Hero...the meaning was clear. Whoever sent the notes—the killer—wanted to kill Hero, too. Why? He swallowed hard.

No. Not going to happen, you son-of-a-bitch. You don't get to decide whether Hero lives or dies. No.

Arturo looked at Imelda, his eyes intense and serious.

"I would die before I let this happen to Hero. I would kill anyone who tried. You have my word, Imelda."

Imelda studied him for a long moment, then stood to go. "You can see Hero. Tonight." She dug in her purse for a scrap of paper. "Here's the address. Don't let me down, Signore Bachi."

"I swear to God, I won't. I won't let you down. More importantly, I won't disappoint Hero."

IMELDA TOLD Hero that Arturo would be picking her up at eight. "Pack an overnight bag. You're staying with him this evening."

Happiness soared in Hero's heart. "He said that?"

"No, I did. I allowed it."

Hero grinned. "Pimp."

"Stop it."

"Big Pimp Sister."

Imelda rolled her eyes. "Are you done?"

Hero hugged her sister. "I am. Thank you, thank you."

"Hero...he seems like a good man, but you're the best judge of that. I showed him those horrible pictures of that girl, Flavia. He agrees with me...you're in danger. But like you, he has no idea who might be targeting you, because he doesn't know who killed his ex-girlfriend. He's convinced it's the same man, and I agree. So, be careful. He's arranged protection for you, and rather annoyingly for me, too, while I'm in the country." Her mouth hitched in a smile. "He's quite tenacious."

HERO TOOK a long soak in Fliss's tub that afternoon and dressed carefully. Her entire body was tingling in anticipation of seeing Arturo, but she was still nervous as hell. When he'd called, she had been beyond elated, but Imelda told her to temper her excitement, and then she insisted on vetting Arturo before she allowed Hero to meet him. Only her newly established relationship with Imelda, as fragile as it was, had made Hero agree to the arrangement.

So now, in a couple of hours, she would see him. The thought of looking into his eyes and feeling his skin against hers...she hoped for it. God, how the hell was she supposed to keep her cool? Hero drew in a shaky breath, opened the window to the balcony of her room, and gazed out over Como. It had been a hot day, but now late in the afternoon, the heat began to dissipate, leaving a sultry feeling.

Hero slid into a light cotton dress of a pale pink and brushed her long hair out. Grinning to herself, she hoped it would get mussed up and tangled before the night was out. She closed her eyes and let the thought of his fingers stroking her bare back make her shiver with anticipation.

BY THE TIME eight o'clock came around, her stomach was in knots. Fliss and Imelda had gone out to dinner. Fliss taking one for the team, as she put it, so Hero was left alone to pace the apartment, getting more and more nervous.

When the intercom buzzed, she started a little, her heart

hammering against her ribs. She paused before opening the door.

The first sight of him, so devastatingly handsome in a dark blue sweater and blue jeans, made her whole body tremble. His eyes gave away his own nerves, but as he opened his mouth to speak, Hero couldn't stop herself. She threw herself into his arms and crushed her mouth against his. His arms clamped around her, his hand cradling the back of her head as he kissed her back, his mouth hungry. Hero's tears wet both their faces.

"I'm sorry. I'm so sorry," Arturo's voice broke as they paused for air, "God, I can't tell you how sorry I am, Hero, *il mia amore*... please forgive me."

"If you'll forgive me, Turo. I'm so sorry about the Patrizzi—about everything." She was weeping with joy at being in his arms. Arturo kissed her again until she couldn't breathe.

"There's nothing to forgive, my sweet darling, nothing. Hero..." He cupped her face in his hands. "I love you. *Ti amo, Ti amo.*"

"I love you, too...I know it's stupid-fast, but I don't care. I *love* you, Arturo Bachi."

He groaned and picked her up. "We'll go to my place, but for now, I can't wait, my love. Where is your bedroom?"

She kissed him as he carried her to her room, then not wanting to wait, they stripped quickly and tumbled onto the bed. Arturo slid his hand down between her legs and smiled. "You're already wet."

"I've been thinking about you—about this—all afternoon. Turo, don't wait. I want you inside of...*oh!*"

With a grin, Arturo thrust his engorged cock deep inside her, and Hero groaned with pleasure. As he thrust, he sucked on her nipples until they were rock-hard, stroked the soft skin of her belly tenderly, attending to every part of her body as if she were the most precious thing in the world. Hero wrapped her legs around his waist, her thighs taut against him, her hands on his face, his shoulders, his back as they made love. She couldn't stop touching him, and when they came—together—they clung to each other as if the world were trying to tear them apart.

"Don't let me go again," she whispered, and he nodded, his eyes closed, his forehead against hers.

"Never again...*never ever again*..."

THEY DRESSED, and Arturo took her hand as they walked to his car. "I have a surprise for you."

Her face was adorably flushed from making love, her hair mussed, her dark eyes shining at him as they drove out of town. Instead of turning south towards his home, he took the north shore road. Hero, her dark hair flying in the night air, laughed. "So, this surprise is...?"

"Patience." He teased her, and she stuck her tongue out at him in jest. Arturo chuckled to himself. It had taken just seconds to get back to where they had been, but no, they seemed to have skipped several steps in their reacquaintance. "Sweet one, I know we have a lot to talk about, and I don't want to miss any of it. But for tonight, can it just be you and I? Just...love?"

Hero touched his face. "I'd like nothing more. We have all the time in the world to talk."

ARTURO TURNED the car into the long driveway of the *Villa Claudia* and waited for Hero's reaction. Hundreds of thousands of tiny white lights had been strewn around the rundown hotel's terrace alongside a few braziers of open flame set along the grounds. Under the pergola, candles guttered on the stone table, and champagne was on ice with two glasses next to it.

Hero blinked a few times and looked at Arturo. He smiled at her. "Do you like it?"

"It's beautiful, Turo, absolutely stunning. Wow...wow..."

Arturo stopped the car, and they got out. He offered her his hand, and slowly they walked up the stone steps to the terrace. Arturo showed her around the grounds first, and then they walked into the hotel. Hero moved around, running her hand over the old-fashioned fixtures, the walls with the peeling wallpaper. "It's incredible," she enthused, "so much character. Is it another hotel?"

Arturo, watching her carefully, shook his head. "No, this is a personal project of mine...and hopefully yours, too."

Hero looked confused. "What do you mean?"

He indicated the hotel. "A home. Our home. If you would do me the honor." He stepped closer to her and cradled her face in his palm. "*Sposami,* Hero Donati. I love you like I've never loved anyone else. Like I'll never love any woman ever again. Marry me. Be my wife."

Hero stared back at him. *It's too soon. We don't know each other. This is crazy.* All of these things played on a loop in her brain, but instead of saying them aloud, she just said one word.

"Yes."

CHAPTER SEVENTEEN

"Married."

Hero nodded her head from side to side. "Sort of. Kind of. Yes. And no."

Imelda looked at Fliss who shrugged, enjoying Imelda's outrage. Imelda ground her teeth. "Hero Donati, are you married to Arturo Bachi or not?"

"Well...yes. Except not legally. Yet. We had our own ceremony last night at our future home. You should see it, Melly, Fliss—it's incredible. It used to be a hotel and..."

"Hero, stop. Slow down." Imelda rubbed her temples. "Are you trying to tell me Arturo proposed, you said yes, and you fake-married him?"

Hero sighed. "Yes, yes, and it wasn't fake. It was real to us. As far as we're concerned, we're married, but we're going to wait a while to make it official. So, we can, you know...get to know each other."

"Right on, girl." Fliss look impressed, but Imelda shook her head.

"You just go from one disaster to another, don't you?" Imelda had clearly reached her limit. "I swear, you get more insane every day. Did you at least talk about some of the problems between you two? Or the fact that a psycho who has already killed once is now targeting you? Because of your relationship—sorry, *marriage* to Arturo Bachi? Do you think that's all just going to magically go away because you got laid and got silly?"

"Wow." Hero's smile vanished. "Melly, do you think you're talking to a three-year-old? Do you really think we didn't talk about it all night? Between the fucking and the silliness, of course. Why do you think we're waiting? Okay, so we're going to call ourselves husband and wife, but we know the mountain we have to climb. I've climbed a few in my life already, you'll recall. We know, Melly. But we're not going to let it stop us from living our lives."

"You may think that your love can conquer all. I'm sure Flavia thought so too before some maniac put a knife in her gut repeatedly. There's someone out there that wants to do the same to you, Hero. Did you forget that?"

"Of course, I didn't fucking forget that!" Hero exploded now, sick of her sister's patronizing. "It's me he wants to kill! Do you think I'm not aware of it every waking second? I might be murdered at any time, and I have no idea why. It could happen today, tomorrow, in five years' time. Am I supposed to put my life on hold until then? This is a good thing for me, Melly. Can't you see that? I love him."

Imelda stared at her for a long time before stalking from the room. Hero and Fliss stared at each other for a few moments, then they heard Imelda come back. She had her suitcase with her. She didn't look at Hero.

"Felicity, thank you again for letting me stay. You have been the most gracious hostess."

Fliss nodded, her eyes wide, not wanting to get between the two sisters. Hero paled, looking at her sister. "Where are you going?"

"Back to the States. I'm clearly not needed here."

"Mel..."

But Imelda was gone. The apartment echoed with the silence. Fliss put her arm around Hero. "Sorry, honey. Look, I have to say, I'm friggin' *delighted* for you."

Hero smiled at her, tears swimming in her eyes. "You are?"

"Hell, yes! I'm all about the romance. But then, I'm young and irresponsible. And it seems to me, Hero, after everything you've been through—you get to be young and irresponsible and live the dream. And Arturo Bachi...you get it, girl. Can I ask something personal?"

Fliss had such a mischievous look on her face that Hero had to nod. "Is he packing? I mean, he looks like he would be *huge*. Give a girl some details."

Hero blushed, but laughed. "Arturo is very blessed in that department."

"Length or girth?"

"Fliss!" But Hero smirked. "*Both.*"

"Lucky bitch."

"Oh, I know. And the stamina of a twenty-year-old."

Fliss groaned. "And the experience of a forty-year-old. Oh, damn you, Hero Donati, you hit the jackpot. And that face of his, too."

"Yup. See this face?" Hero, cheered by Fliss's banter, pointed at her smile. "Smug."

"Smuggysmugginess."

"You know it." Hero looked at her watch. "Well, he's coming to pick me up in a half-hour. Want to meet my husband officially?"

ARTURO'S SMILE hadn't left his face from the moment Hero said yes until now, when he told Peter. Peter sighed smiled and shook his head. "I might have known. You're both so impetuous, you deserve each other. Congratulations, my friend. Did you settle everything else between you?"

"The apartment is water under the bridge. I should never have been so obsessed with it in the first place. It's just bricks and mortar."

Peter frowned. "No, it was your dream, Turo. Your business. But anyway, it doesn't matter now. Did you tell her the name of the new hotel?"

"No, that's a surprise for another day. I took her to Villa Claudia."

"Marcella told me. She said she'd never strung so many Christmas lights at one time."

Arturo laughed. "Marcie is a wonder. She'll see my thanks in her paycheck. It looked amazing and the whole night was...unforgettable."

Peter smiled. "I've never seen you this besotted. Not even with...Flavia."

Arturo looked down at his coffee for a long moment. "If it's possible, I love Hero even more. They could be sisters in looks, but they are a million miles apart in character. Hero is goofy and funny, Flavia was more serious and..." He trailed off.

"Self-involved." Peter's voice was harsh. "Time for the truth about Flavia, Arturo. We already know she was cheating on you."

Arturo nodded, reluctantly accepting what he'd always dodged in his memories. "Flav used her looks to get whatever she wanted. Hero's not like that. Not even slightly. She doesn't use people for any reason."

Peter studied his friend. "But Flav's killer is now targeting Hero. Which leads me to ask...why didn't he kill her at the Patrizzi? He had her alone and vulnerable and, *Jesus*, the girl's tiny."

"I don't know. Unless..."

"Unless what?"

"No. Never mind." Arturo sighed. "Look, I have to go pick her up...she'll be moving into my place as soon as she's ready. Which I hope is now, but I'm trying to hold back."

Peter didn't smile. "Sure, I could tell with this whole 'we're husband and wife' thing."

"Unofficially," but Arturo grinned. "I cannot wait until we *do* make it official."

"Turo."

Arturo shrugged. "I'm in love, brother. I'm not apologizing for that."

HERO WAS STUFFING the last of her clothes into her case while Fliss sat on the guest bed, pouting. "I'm going to miss having you here."

"I won't be far, and I'll still come help out in the store. If Arturo thinks I'm going to be a stay-at-home wifey, he'll have another thing coming. And hey, when we start on Villa Claudia, I'll need your artistic skills."

Her cell phone rang, and Fliss hopped off the bed. "I'll give you some privacy."

Hero was smiling when she answered the phone, not even checking who was calling. "Hello?"

"Hero Donati?"

"That's me."

A low chuckle. Immediately Hero's hackles went up. "Can I help you?"

"Can you help me? Well, let's see, beautiful."

She frowned, not placing the voice or even the accent. It was being disguised somehow. "Who are you?"

Another laugh. "Your killer, Hero. The person who's going to gut you."

Her blood froze. "Why are you doing this?"

"Doing what? Calling you? I wanted to hear your lovely voice, of course. And to tell you in exquisite detail how I'm going to end your life. I'm so looking forward to it."

Hero got angry. "You son-of-a-bitch! Do you honestly think I'm going to sit back and—"

"*Shut your filthy mouth, whore!*" The sudden change from an almost whisper to a roar of anger silenced Hero. She was trembling. She checked the caller ID. Blocked. Of course.

"Look, I don't know why you've decided to fixate on me. I don't know many people here, and I don't think I've done anything to you, whoever you are. You should know, I have protection."

"Oh, I know. It won't be enough to stop me. I'm going to gut you slowly, beautiful one; it'll be much, much more drawn out than when I killed Flavia. You will beg me to kill you because the pain will be unbearable, but I'm going to watch you bleed out, and I'll enjoy every moment."

Hero gritted her teeth. "Then come at me, bro. Who's to say I won't kill you first?"

She ended the call and almost threw the phone across the room, but she stopped herself. *No. Calm down. It's what he wants.*

Instead, she checked her watch. Arturo would be with her in a few moments. She sucked in a breath and grabbed her things.

Fliss was waiting in the living room with two glasses of sparkling wine. "Just to celebrate our brief time as roommates."

Hero hugged her. "You are a true friend, Fliss. I'll get the movers to pick the rest of my stuff up as soon as I can get it organized."

"No problem. Just don't forget me."

"Never gonna' happen."

. . .

HE GRINNED to himself as he heard the phone line go dead. That should ruin her evening with the bastard. God, he couldn't wait to carve her up, but this...the anticipation was just as sweet. After all, he couldn't kill her twice, although because she looked so much like Flavia, it was kind of like reliving that glorious night.

It had been a pity Flavia had died so quickly. Because of the party going on just yards away, he'd had to stab her quickly and brutally before she could scream or anyone else came close. Hero Donati would suffer much more. He would slide the knife into her and leave it buried inside her as she bled slowly to death. Then as she was close to death, he would go to town, stab her quickly many, many times over. *Butcher* her. And then he would allow Arturo to find her body and know that he had lost. Again.

If Flavia's death had almost made him insane, Hero's murder would destroy him entirely.

He couldn't wait.

CHAPTER EIGHTEEN

Hero told Arturo about the call. "I don't want it to spoil our evening, but we agreed. No more secrets."

Arturo was angry. "*Figlia di puttana!*" He pulled her into his arms. "You're safe, you know? I won't let him hurt you again, Hero. I swear it."

"I do know." Hero kissed him. "But, Arturo, I think we need to up the ante on finding this asshole. We can't be passive."

"Agreed. Look, let's go to my place and make a plan. We'll call in every detective we can, go to the polizia—not that I think they will be much help."

"Well, we'll try everything. It's not like either of us can't afford good security, but I don't want to live looking over my shoulder. Fuck that."

Arturo smiled at her. "I love your dirty mouth."

"It'll be wrapped around your cock soon, if you keep talking like that."

"I'll make you keep that promise, *bella*."

She kissed him until they had to break for air. "Let's go home, baby, and fuck ourselves silly. There's time enough to be super-cops tomorrow."

Arturo groaned as he slid into the driver's seat of the car. "What you do to me, Hero Donati..."

She grinned at him. "Drive fast, Bachi."

"Okay." Hero set down her laptop on the table in front of Arturo the next morning. "My best chance for help is via the US Consulate. If we can get the Como police to provide us with their reports of my attack and the time I went to them with the notes, then we're good to go."

Arturo nodded. "Good. What will the Consulate do?"

"Well, we'll still have to investigate for ourselves; they won't do that. But they have more pull in getting information that we may not have access to. So, here's what I think. The nearest consulate is in Milan. We go, tell them our story, and ask what resources they have to help us. Then we let the local polizia know that the US State Department knows about the case. That might make them take it a little more seriously."

"I agree. For my part, I've been thinking we need to go see my uncle. First, because he's a sick man, and I would like him to meet you before...well, you know. He's also a little odd... but he's really good at not letting emotion cloud his judgment. A little too good, maybe. If he can see the details of this in his dispassionate way, he might see something we can't."

"Such as?"

Arturo hesitated. "Perhaps someone who works for us who might be more involved than we think."

Hero's eyes opened wide, and she sat down heavily on the chair next to him. "Turo...you don't mean Peter, surely?"

"I hope not. God, I hope not, but something's been bugging me lately. It may be nothing, and I hope to God, it isn't anything, but I keep going back to the night Flavia was murdered. When I got to the party, Peter had already left.

George was still there, though; he was the one who told me Flavia was missing."

"Had Peter ever been aggressive towards Flavia?"

Arturo smiled slightly. "Peter's never been aggressive to anyone, as far as I know."

Hero shook her head. "I don't know where this is coming from. Granted, I don't know Peter as well as you, but Turo, surely out of anyone, even me, he's the person you trust the most."

He looked at her for a long moment. "You're right. I'm just being paranoid."

Hero smiled at him. "I think you are, baby. Let's not throw suspicion on someone we know is on our side."

But Arturo wasn't convinced. When he met his friend later at the office, Peter seemed cool towards him, and Arturo finally asked him outright. "What's going on with you, Pete? Have I offended you in some way?"

Peter sighed. "No, Turo. No, it's just...I'm wary. You tell me Hero is getting threats, and her life is in danger, and I can't help but be worried that if something does happen to her, you won't survive it. And if you don't survive, neither will I. You're my brother, Turo, my family. I was there last time, when you so nearly lost the will to live. It was...horrific. I don't want you to go through that again. And hell, I don't want to go through it again either. Once was enough for five lifetimes."

Arturo felt a wash of guilt over him. "Nothing is going to happen to Hero, Peter. We're dealing with it, both of us, and we could use your help. We're going to find out who killed Flavia, and who is threatening Hero and why."

"You're the common thread, Turo," Peter pointed out. "I'm concerned for you. I worry that whoever it is, they're setting you up, especially now that your uncle is dying. Think of the morality clause in your father's will...Arturo, if something does happen to Hero and you're arrested, you forfeit everything. Everything."

Arturo nodded. "I know. Pete, believe me when I say that without Hero, nothing would mean much to me anymore. I frankly don't care."

"Which is all very noble and romantic, but this is the real world."

Arturo sighed. "Peter, even without the company and my father's fortune, I have more money than I need."

"A lot of it is tied up, Turo. Your cash in hand is a lot less than the figures might indicate."

Arturo shrugged. "I leave that up to you, Peter. If I lose it all, I still have everything if Hero is safe with me." He studied his friend. "There's something else, isn't there? Do you not like Hero?"

Peter hesitated. "I don't want to keep mentioning it, but she looks so much like Flavia. I...keep seeing Hero ending up like Flavia."

Arturo winced. "Believe me, Pete, I see that image every day. Every day. But Hero's a fighter. She's not going to take this lying down. Will you help us?"

"Of course. *Of course.* And for the record, I do like Hero. I like her very much. I just feel like you two are on a tightrope, and if she falls, it'll end you."

"Then we won't fall, Pete. It's that simple."

"I hope you're right, Turo," Peter said quietly. "I really do."

HERO TRIED Imelda's number again and got her voicemail... again. She hated the way she had left things with her sister, especially after they had begun to find a new peace between them. Hero rubbed her face and ended the call without leaving another message. Instead, she called her Mom in Kenosha.

"Darling, how wonderful to hear your voice." Deirdre Donati's soft voice made Hero want to cry. "How are you?"

"I'm good, Ma, really good. How're you? How's Dad?"

"Your Dad is doing great now, honey. He's just sulking because I won't allow him fried chicken anymore." Her mom laughed, and Hero felt a wash of both fondness and sadness.

"I miss you, Ma."

"We both miss you terribly, Hero, my darling, but I hear you have a new man in your life?"

Hero told her about Arturo, messaging her mother a photograph. "Oh my," Deirdre said with a chuckle, "I might have to fight you for him, Hero. What a pretty boy."

Hero laughed aloud. "You are incorrigible, Ma. I can't wait for you to meet him." Her smile faded. "Ma...have you heard from Melly?"

Her mother sighed. "No, darling, I'm sorry. You know what Melly is like when she's in a snit. Gone to ground. She called from the Milan airport but since then...nothing. I'll leave it a few more days, then I'll do the Mom thing and yell at her."

"Don't yell too hard, Ma. It's my fault, really. She was just looking out for me." Hero felt tearful again. She hadn't told her mother about the death threats, especially after her father's health scare. There was no point in panicking the rest of her family. "Tell her I love her, would you? I love her, and I'm sorry."

"I will, sweetheart. We love you very much, Hero. Remember that."

"I love you, too, Ma, so much. Give Dad a kiss from me."

AFTER SHE ENDED THE CALL, Hero felt a little more positive. She went to find her bodyguard and found him in the kitchen drinking coffee. Gaudio was a hulking Italian, his dark hair slicked back, his brow heavy and brooding. He looked terrifying, but Hero had liked the man as soon as Arturo introduced them. Gaudio might look scary to anyone attacking her, but Arturo trusted him, so Hero had no trouble in believing Gaudio would keep her safe.

She had also hatched a plan that was a million miles away from the reality of her stalker. "Gaudio, I'd like to go into town today—go see my friend, Fliss. Can we make that happen?"

"No problem, Piccolo."

Hero smiled. She loved the informality of Gaudio's personality. It made having a guard so much easier on her.

They drove into Como late morning. It was a cloudless day, and Hero let the sun soak into her skin. *So much darkness*, she thought, *and yet this place is so beautiful, so full of possibility*.

Fliss threw her arms around her. "It's been two whole weeks," she accused a grinning Hero. "Please tell me you at least spent all that time shagging that gorgeous man of yours?"

"Um…Fliss, this is Gaudio. Gaudio, my good friend Fliss."

Fliss looked the gigantic man up and down appreciatively. "I might have to get myself a stalker if it means getting one of you. Hello."

Gaudio's white, even teeth shone through his thick beard. "Hello, ma'am."

"God, no, it's Fliss. Ma'am is my mum. Or the Queen." She winked at Hero who chuckled and moved towards the staff room at the back.

"How about you two talk, and I'll make some coffee?" Hero said.

Smiling, she left them alone and made herself busy with the coffee machine, one ear on the conversation. She'd had the idea last night: Gaudio and Fliss shared the same goofy sense of humor. She'd said as much to Arturo, who rolled his eyes.

"Matchmaking?"

"Hell, yes."

Now, she waited for the coffee to steep. She noticed an envelope with her name on it, thrown on the table along with some other mail. Her stomach constricted a little. Her name was typed neatly on the expensive looking paper. She picked it up by the edges, then, curiosity getting the better of her, handled it with some tissues as she opened it. Her shoulders slumped with relief. An invitation, printed on heavy cardstock.

Miss Hero Donati plus her chosen guest are formally invited to the Summer's Eve party at Villa Charlotte as a special guest of Signore George Galiano.
RSVP.

"*Chosen guest.*" He meant Arturo. "George, you are an *ass*," she said to herself. She threw the card back onto the table, then changed her mind. Maybe Arturo would get a kick out of it. She stuck the card in her purse, then took the coffee through to her friends.

She winked at Fliss. "So, you two going out or what?"

"You're as subtle as a sledgehammer," Fliss said, not even slightly embarrassed. "Just so happens, Gee and I like the same kind of movies."

'*Gee*' already? Hero grinned at her bodyguard and had just opened her mouth to speak as the window behind them exploded, and all hell broke loose.

CHAPTER NINETEEN

Arturo drove like a madman into Como, seeing the crowds of shocked-looking people, the police, the ambulances. "*Mio Dio...*"

He parked the car as close as he could to the store, and then ran the rest of the way. There was a police cordon, but Arturo ignored it, ducking under the tape. He could see Gaudio, Fliss, and—*thank God*—Hero standing talking to the police. She saw him, and he rushed over and wrapped his arms around her. "Are you alright? *Cara mia,* are you hurt?" he demanded over and over again, in between frantic kisses.

"Totally fine," she reassured him. "Just shaken. We're all okay." She looked up at him. "It was a busted gas line, nothing sinister. The restaurant across the street is pretty messed up, and there's some people hurt, but no one was killed."

"*Mio Dio, mio Dio*...when I heard, I thought..."

"Yeah. Me, too," she admitted. "I thought that was it. But I'm still here. Gaudio threw himself on top of Fliss and I. He got a little cut up from the window blowing in, but he's been a big brave boy about it."

He knew she was joking to make him relax, and he smiled down at her. "I love you. Come on, let me go thank Gaudio."

They found the big man surrounded by paramedics, waving them away like so many flies as they inspect his myriad cuts.

Arturo grasped the bodyguard's uninjured hand and wrung it firmly. "*Grazie,* Gaudio. I owe you big time."

"Just doing my job, boss." Gaudio winked and grinned at Fliss, who mock-slapped him.

"The things you will do to get a grope in. Come on, Gee, let's go see the damage."

Gaudio looked at Arturo, who, his arms securely around Hero, nodded.

Hero smiled up at him. "Thank you for getting here so fast."

"Think I broke all the traffic laws, but just so you know, I'd break them all happily anytime."

Hero brushed her lips against his. "Do you have to go back to work?"

"Feeling frisky?"

"That whole adrenaline thing."

Arturo laughed. "I think I'm married to a nympho."

Hero giggled. "You made me a nympho, Bachi."

Arturo grinned and took her hand. "Come on. I have a plan."

The car climbed into the mountains until they reached a small plateau. "Not many people come up here," Arturo told her, "so we should have the place to ourselves."

It was cooler—a *lot* cooler—in the mountains, but Hero didn't care. She unbuckled her seat belt and straddled Arturo. "Making out like teenagers in the car," she murmured, her lips against his.

"We'll be doing much, much more than teenagers do, *cara mia*, believe me..."

He slid his hands under her T-shirt, his green eyes full of fire and intensity. "Do you like this T-shirt, *Bella*?"

Hero shook her head. "Not particularly."

"Good."

He tore her T-shirt open, the quick shock of it and the cold air on her skin making Hero gasp. Arturo pulled the lacy cup of her bra down and took her nipple into his mouth hungrily, sucking and teasing it.

Hero ground against his groin, then unzipped his fly, reaching to release his straining cock, stroking the hot length of it as Arturo attacked her other nipple. Hero pulled her panties to one side and impaled herself on his cock, sighing as the thick length penetrated her.

"*Mio Dio*, Hero..." Arturo groaned as she began to thrust herself onto him. The confinement of the vehicle only made their lovemaking more intimate, skin on skin, gazes locked, their breath mingling as they kissed.

"I love you," Hero whispered, "I've never loved any man as much as I love you, Arturo Bachi."

He closed his eyes, nodding to himself, utterly absorbed in her. "As I love you, my precious darling. Please...don't ever leave me...promise me, promise me."

"I promise..." Hero managed to get the words out before her orgasm robbed her of her speech and her head dropped back as she gasped. Arturo kissed her throat then groaned as he came, pumping thick creamy cum deep into her belly.

"Hero...*Hero*..."

ON THE DRIVE back to Arturo's home, they joked around with each other, teasing, sharing intimate smiles and knowing looks. Arturo lifted her hand to his lips. "Is it wrong that I kind of hope we made a baby?"

Hero was shocked that she felt no fear when he said that. Not even the memory of Beth changed the peace that she suddenly felt. She would always love her little girl, but that didn't mean she couldn't love another baby just as much. "No, because I would love that, too."

If she stopped to think how much her life had changed in just a few weeks, she would get scared, but all she knew right now was that this man was her future, and if she were to get pregnant, she knew it would only solidify that for her.

However, when they got back to Villa Bachi, everything changed. Waiting for them was Peter and a man they didn't recognize. Peter introduced them.

"Turo, Hero, this is Simon Lascelles. He's from the American Consulate in Milan. Mr. Lascelles, Arturo Bachi, and Hero Donati. I think we had better go inside."

Hero shot a worried look at Arturo, who squeezed her hand and nodded. "Let's."

Inside, Simon Lascelles sat down with them. "Miss Donati, I'm aware you contacted us a few days ago about the threats to your life. While we have been looking into them, we discovered something rather disturbing."

Hero's chest tightened. "What is it?"

"You were kind enough to give us your family's details, and we checked their wellbeing as a matter of routine."

"Oh, God. Mom...Dad..."

"They're fine," Lascelles assured her quickly. "It's your adoptive sister. You told us she left Milan to fly home?"

Hero couldn't speak. "Oh, God."

Lascelles nodded. "I'm afraid we have confirmed it. Miss Imelda Donati never made the flight. She never left Italy."

Arturo talked to Lascelles and Peter as they left, but Hero

couldn't hear anymore. She dropped her head into her hands. Why? Why go after Imelda?

Her cell phone rang, and she knew immediately who it was. "Where the fuck is my sister?"

Her tormenter laughed. "Safe. For now. She'll be released right after my knife guts you."

"Why are you doing this? What have I ever done to you?" Her voice was a whisper now, the pain of knowing he had her sister overwhelming her.

There was a long pause, and when he spoke again, his voice was so full of malice and malevolence that it made her shiver. "Because you love *him*..."

The line went dead.

ARTURO CAME BACK into the room then and saw her defeated look, the phone on the floor. Hero looked up at him, the pain in her eyes palpable, and it made his chest hurt.

"*Il mia amore*, what is it?" But she just shook her head, unable to speak.

He sat down next to her and wrapped his arms around her, feeling her tremble. "He called you again, didn't he?"

"He has Imelda," she whispered into his chest. "He says she'll be released after I'm dead. He won't release her. He'll kill her, too."

"He is not going to kill *anyone*." Arturo felt a murderous rage of his own. "We're going to find out who this motherfucker is and end him, once and for all."

Hero looked up at him and nodded. "Agreed. Any clue how to do it?"

Arturo felt hopelessness seep into his bones. "No. But we'll figure it out." He stroked her hair away from her face. "Just promise me you won't ever give up."

"I promise. We will get to have our happy ever after, Turo."

"Yes, we do. Damn right we will."

"And we'll get my sister back safe and sound?"

The hopeful, trusting look she gave him melted Arturo completely, and he drew her back into a tender kiss. "Yes. I promise, *cara mia*. We will stop at nothing to ensure her safety. And yours."

No matter how much Arturo spent on detectives or leaned on the local polizia or the American consulate, no one could tell them anything.

One afternoon they sat in his office with notepads in front of them and stared at each other.

"Look, I know with the police we've been through anyone that would hold a grudge against us, but I think we have to do it again. *Everything*. Ex-girlfriends and boyfriends, one-night stands, old schoolfriends or enemies. If it's just a random psychopath, then there's not a lot anyone can do."

Hero nodded. The strain of knowing her sister was out there, in pain, in such terrible danger, had gotten to her, and now Arturo saw the violet shadows underneath her eyes. It had been a week since they'd discovered Imelda's abduction, and there was nothing. No one had seen her; it was as if she had vanished into thin air. "Okay, so we go into our histories. School days."

"School days…if I'm honest, school days for me were about one person. Flavia. We met when we were in seventh grade. Every boy wanted her. But I got lucky. Or, unlucky."

Hero frowned. "Why do you say that?"

"Because, looking back now, Flavia always got her own way. In everything. I've only really begun to remember it that way since I met you. Not that I'm comparing you."

Hero smiled at him. "I know. But the comparison is there,

though: our similar looks, the fact that we both loved you, the fact that someone wants to kill me the same way he says he killed her."

"Why do you say it like that? He *says* he killed Flav?"

"Because what if this isn't about Flavia or me," Hero asked, "but about you—and not in an obsessive, jealous way? What if this is about business? About sending you over the edge? Your uncle is sick, dying. You're about to become one of the richest men in Italy, possibly even the world, and the scope of the business you're about to inherit—it boggles the mind. What if this crap is all about unsettling you?"

"It's working," Arturo said darkly and sighed. "So, you think that maybe Flav's murder is entirely separate?"

"I don't know," Hero shook her head, "but it's an option we should look into. A copycat. Maybe they think killing me will destroy you."

"Then they'd be right. Why take your sister?"

"Obviously they know about the extra protection I have. They know I'd give myself up in a heartbeat to save Melly."

"*Mio Dio.*" Arturo closed his eyes. "Please don't say things like that."

"You would do the same," Hero said gently, reaching out and stroking his face, "you know you would."

He caught her hand with his, pressing it to his face. "Then we'll just have to be ruthless in who we investigate. That means everyone. Staring with that *figlia di puttana*, George Galiano."

Hero nodded. "He is a creep, no doubt. But something cautions me about really going after him. He's too obvious a suspect. He's like a comedy villain. Like the Hooded Claw."

Arturo raised his eyebrows. "Who?"

Hero chuckled. "Never mind. But, here's a thought...we could always try a bait and switch."

"How do you mean?"

"We should break up."

"What the hell are you talking about?" He had gone cold at her words, but she was smiling.

"Not for real, obviously. But, we should argue, publicly...and make sure George sees it. He'll try and slide in, I guarantee it. Sorry if that makes me sound arrogant, but he's the type. He would love to seduce me to get back at you."

"Using yourself as bait?" He grimaced in disgust. "No way."

"Not bait. There's no way I'm going to do anything with him, but if he has a conversation with 'angry me,' I can gauge his level of..." She searched for the word. "Violence."

Arturo shook his head, but Hero held up her hand. "Wait, let me explain. By that I mean, a woman can tell when a man has sex on his mind or something more sinister. We have an built-in radar for this stuff—most of the time. I can't even explain it. We women almost always have to deal with sex pests or men who can turn violent even if all we've done is politely refuse a drink. It takes a very sneaky man to hide that—and George isn't that bright."

"This all seems very based on..."

"Gut instinct. That's right. Provable in court? Nope, but I'll get a read on whether George is capable of killing me or if he just wants to fuck me."

Arturo got up and paced around, cursing under his breath in Italian.

Hero caught his hands with hers. "We do it somewhere public, where people can see us really duking it out. We can get one of your detectives to follow George, to see when he goes to lunch, then we perform our little play. I'll cry a lot. George won't be able to conceal his glee. He'll want to be the white knight. We'll let him. Then we get a read."

Arturo stared at Hero unhappily, and she returned his gaze steadily. "I don't like this."

"It'll all be totally in public."

"What if he wants you to go somewhere else with him? If you say no, he'll get suspicious, I'm telling you."

Hero took a deep breath in. "Then we'll have a detective follow me."

Arturo closed his eyes. He was haunted by the image of Hero, in a pool of her own blood, her belly torn open, her eyes closed forever.

Stop it.

"No. There are too many things that can go wrong."

"Turo." Hero stood and put her arms around him. "He, whoever he is, has my sister and the police have no clues. We have to do this. We have to investigate every one of our friends and colleagues one by one. No one is going to help us with this."

Arturo pulled her close. "If anything happens to you…"

"It won't. I'm pretty scrappy. The dude in the Patrizzi apartment…I just didn't see him coming. This way, we're tackling it head on. We're prepared."

Arturo tangled his fingers in her hair and was silent for a long moment. "Promise you won't put yourself in danger."

"No more than I have to."

"It takes a second, a momentary lapse, and then you're bleeding out, and I lose you forever."

"Not going to happen." Hero nodded confidently, and Arturo knew she would not be persuaded otherwise.

CHAPTER TWENTY

George Galiano looked up from his newspaper to see Hero Donati stalk into the restaurant, followed by an angry-looking Arturo. Arturo grabbed her arm, and she whirled around on him. "*Don't.* I told you, it's over! Leave me alone!"

"Please don't do this, Hero, I love you...I'm sorry."

Hero pushed Arturo away as he reached for her. "No...I don't want this. Please, leave me alone...please..." She began to cry, and Arturo ran his hand through his dark curls. He looked utterly destroyed.

"I can't believe this is over..."

Hero shook her head, tears pouring down her lovely face. "It should never have started."

Arturo stared at her for a moment longer, then turned on his heel and stalked out.

Well, well, well.

George made sure he was the first one to approach a sobbing Hero, steering her into a private booth. "*Bella*, please, sit down and calm yourself. Could we have a brandy over here, please?"

He smiled at a worried-looking waitress who nodded and took off.

He sat down next to Hero, his arm around her trembling body. He stroked her long dark hair back over her shoulder. "Come now, lovely Hero, please don't cry."

"It's over, it's over..." She kept repeating and shaking her head, but finally, he got her to take a few deep breaths and calm herself. She sipped the brandy he had ordered her.

"Okay?"

"God, I'm so sorry...thank you, George. What must people think of me? It's just..."

George smiled at her, taking her hand. "What happened?"

She met his gaze. "He was...getting too possessive. I'm not sure if I should tell you this but...I've been getting threats. Death threats."

"*Mio Dio, no.*"

Hero nodded. "They—whoever they are—have taken my sister. I'm supposed to hand myself over to whoever it is, and they'll let her go."

"And you?"

She met his gaze, the terror in her lovely brown eyes searing. "I'll be killed."

"But why for heaven's sake?"

She shook her head, tears dropping down her cheeks. "I don't know. I don't know."

"And Bachi is what? Telling you how to run your life?"

"He said...God...I don't even think he meant it now, but just hearing the words come out of his mouth..."

"Tell me." George leaned forward, and she searched his eyes.

"He said...if it meant me dying, he...would let Imelda die."

George sat back, sucking in a deep breath. "I can see his point, but you still must have been shocked."

"I was. I challenged him...and that's when things got bad. He practically wanted me to be a prisoner in my own—hell, not even my *own* home, but *his*. He took my phone, wouldn't let me call my parents in the US...the last week has been nothing short of hell. God, I really shouldn't be telling you this. I should go."

Hero stood, flustered and flushed, but George caught her hand. "No, don't go. At least until you've calmed down. I can find you somewhere to stay tonight."

"No, really, it's fine. Thank you."

"Hero." George stood, dwarfing her tiny frame. "Allow me to help. However much you might think it, this is not a safe place for a beautiful woman on her own."

Hero looked wary for a moment, then her shoulders slumped. "Fine."

She allowed him to steer her out of the restaurant and into his car. "I'll take you to a hotel outside of town. That way, you can find some peace."

"Thank you." She still seemed a little nervous, looking around as they pulled away from the sidewalk. George kept glancing over at her. Was she scared that Arturo might see them? Was she scared of him?

He smiled to himself. He had waited weeks for this moment, to be alone with her, vulnerable and distressed. He tapped in a number on his cell phone, switching it to hands-free as he drove. "Yes, this is George Galiano. I need your best hotel suite. Yes... today. I have a friend in need of it. Thank you, we'll be there directly."

He ended the call and looked at Hero, who was calmer now and silent. She looked pale. "The Villa Helena has a suite for you."

"I can't thank you enough."

"I'll arrange for your things to be brought over from *Villa Bachi*."

Hero sighed. "I never thought when I came here that this would be my life."

George put his hand on hers, and she stiffened but didn't pull away. "I believe I've said this to you before, Hero. Arturo Bachi isn't your only option."

Hero didn't say anything then. After he'd installed her in the suite at the Villa Helena, he kissed her hand and left her alone. Going down to reception, he slid a one-hundred euro note to the receptionist, a cute young blonde who he'd fucked on more than one occasion. "I want to know her every movement, every phone call out, everything. If she has any visitors," he said, and the blonde nodded, simpering at him. He'd take her out as thanks, plow that sweet cunt of hers, and pretend she was Hero. Soon, he wouldn't have to pretend.

Because George Galiano always, always got what he wanted, and by God, he wanted Hero Donati, and he would do anything to have her, even if it meant taking her against her will.

CHAPTER TWENTY-ONE

"He's having you watched by the hotel staff."

Hero sighed. "I thought as much. Did he send one of his goons for my clothes?"

Arturo laughed darkly. "He wouldn't dare. He'll come himself to rub my nose in it."

"God, he's such a creep."

"I'm sorry, baby. Look, we can call this off anytime, you know that."

Hero smiled down at the burner phone she was using. "I do know that, but while Melly is still missing, I'll do anything. Turo," she faltered a little, "getting a read on George might mean…me going along with what he wants…to a point of course."

Arturo was silent, and Hero felt her heart clench. "Baby, I love you, only you. But I might need to appear to be…God…submitting to his 'charms.' So gross."

Arturo gave a half-laugh, and she relaxed a little. "Be careful, Hero, I couldn't bear the thought of him touching you. What's your read on him so far?"

"Creepy asshole, hates you, wants to fuck me just because

I'm yours—or, to his knowledge, your ex. Following my gut? I just don't know yet. I need to get a little more information. See if he gives anything up."

"*Mio Dio,*" Arturo sighed. "Do what you have to do, *cara mia,* but please, take care."

"I will. What's your plan?"

"Going to my uncle. Besides you, he's the only person I trust to be honest with me."

Hero bit her lip. "You're going to talk to him about Pete?"

"Yep. God, I hate, hate, *hate* that I have to question my oldest friend's motives. He's been nothing but a rock to me."

"I know, baby, I'm sorry."

"But, like you, I have to follow my gut, if only to rule him out."

She sighed. "I know."

"Listen, the rooms next to your suite have my people in them. You get scared at all—scream. They'll be right there."

Hero sighed. "God, I miss you already."

"And I you, my darling. Do we really have any idea what we're doing?"

Hero gave a half-sob, half-laugh. "No. But we have to do something, and this is it."

"I know. You should hear some of the ridiculous notions going around my head about who could be targeting you and me."

"Like?"

Arturo hesitated. "Like...Tom. What if he faked his death? What if...*blah blah blah.* You see? Ridiculous—and I feel bad for even thinking that about your husband. I'm sorry."

"No, I get it. I'm having crazy thoughts like that as well. I didn't get to see Tom and Beth buried, so there's always going to be that lack of closure for me. But they're just that—crazy thoughts. ...And Arturo?"

"Yes, *cara mia*?"

"*You* are my husband now."

Arturo laughed, a deep, rich sound which warmed her soul. "You bet I am. I love you."

"I love you, baby. Sleep well."

"Goodnight, *il mia amore*."

ARTURO WASN'T surprised when George Galiano showed up at Villa Bachi the next morning. George's smile was insidious.

"I come on behalf of a friend to ask you to send her belongings on to her. She asked that I take possession of them as she doesn't wish for you to know where she is."

Arturo ground his teeth together and had to remind himself this was all a ruse, or else he would have punched the smug smile off of George's face. "Drop the bullshit, Galiano. Hero can fight her own battles; she doesn't need you."

George smirked a little. "You abandoned her in tears in a restaurant. She's utterly humiliated."

"And what do you know about Hero? You've spoken what? Three times since she's been here? Stay out of things which don't concern you, George. Now, are you going to tell me where she is?"

"No, I think she'd rather you didn't know. From what I hear, she's already going through a tough time."

Arturo went very still. "And what do you know about that?"

George smiled. "Hero told me everything. Seems you just can't keep your women safe, can you, Bachi? First Flavia, now Hero."

"Nothing is going to happen to Hero." Arturo kept his cool, but his knuckles were going white as he curled his hands into fists.

"I certainly hope not. What a waste it would be, such beauty. This community couldn't take another tragedy."

George was enjoying this, but Arturo couldn't tell whether his enjoyment was from goading Arturo or from the thought of hurting Hero. He prayed it was the former.

"What do you want, George?"

George's smile disappeared. "Nothing you could give me. I've come to expect nothing from you. As should that lovely girl. You're a cancer, Bachi. You ruin lives. You deserve every bit of pain that comes to you. Maybe Hero *would* be better off dead."

Arturo lunged for him. George sidestepped him neatly, and Arturo went sprawling. As he clambered to his feet, George chuckled. "You know what, Bachi? My mission from now on will be to poison lovely Hero against you. Given the state she was in yesterday, it'll be a cakewalk. You'll see. That beauty will be in my bed soon enough, and once again, you'll be left with nothing. Any wonder your women always choose me?"

He stalked out, and Arturo heard him laugh as he left the house. Arturo got to his feet slowly, dusting himself off. It had taken all of his will to fake that lunge, send himself sprawling to the floor, humiliating himself in front of his old enemy.

He picked up the burner phone and called his wife. "He bought it," he said and began to smile.

"My dear, I'm afraid I don't think Bachi will be sending your belongings to you. He's behaving like a child, petulant and selfish—as always."

Hero nodded, sighing. "Well, it was only clothes, George. There are plenty of stores. I'd rather not risk a confrontation with him. I'd rather not see him at all."

George sat down on the suite's couch. Hero took a seat opposite him. "You've been very kind, George. I can't thank you enough. I just have to figure out what my next move will be."

He nodded. "I would like to help you if you'll allow. Perhaps we could send out some detectives to find where your sister is being held."

Hero's heart began to thud a little quicker. "Arturo already did that. There was no sign of her around Como or Milan."

"Perhaps Bachi doesn't have the contacts I do." George's smile was snake-like, and Hero felt a cold shot of adrenaline through her stomach.

Careful, careful now...

"What do you mean?"

"I mean...he is more...*discerning* about who his business contacts are. I'm not naïve like him. I go where the money is and sometimes that means..."

"The underworld. Why would someone in the underworld want me dead?"

George studied her, his eyes like gimlets. "There is *always* a good reason to kill a beautiful woman, Hero."

His words felt like a knife in her gut. *Ironic,* she thought, *seeing as he is now my number one suspect for wanting to knife me in the gut.* "Would *you* kill me, George?" Her voice was soft.

His expression changed immediately. "My dearest Hero, *no,* that is not what I meant! I wasn't talking about myself, rather, the world in general." He sighed. "So much jealousy in this world, so much entitlement. 'She is mine. If I can't have her, no one can, etcetera, etcetera.' We see it every day on our television news. Dear one, no, I only meant...there doesn't appear to a limit to the reasons why."

Huh. He had a point, but it still made her feel sick. In a flash, he was sitting next to her. She tried not to flinch as he stroked her hair back behind her ear. His eyes were intent on hers, and she looked back steadily.

"You are truly exquisite," he murmured. "It would be a tragedy if any harm befell you, Hero Donati. A tragedy. I will not let that happen."

Oh, God, he's going to kiss me. Go along with it. Fake it. Don't throw up. But instead, George picked up her hand and kissed the back of it. She breathed out shakily, letting him hear her nerves, hoping he would think it was desire.

His arrogance won out. "Darling one, I will call on you... later. If I may, that is? For supper?"

She forced a smile on her face. "Sure."

He did kiss her then, just a light brushing of lips against hers. Hero clenched her fists but didn't pull away. "Later, then." His voice was full of meaning.

Hero smiled. "Later."

She waited until he had closed the door and heard the elevator ping down the corridor, before she scooted out and knocked on the room next to hers. Gaudio opened the door.

"Hey there." His big grin made her feel a lot more secure.

"Got a problem," Hero said after hugging him. "I might need you to do some serious acting for me tonight to get me out of, well, um...having to sleep with George Galiano."

As Gaudio's eyes opened wide, she grinned and nodded to a chair. "Have a seat. This might take some planning."

"No fucking way."

Hero chuckled. "There's no way I'm actually going to go through with it. I've worked it out with Gaudio. He's going to interrupt at the appropriate moment."

Arturo sighed. "I hate this. I hate not being with you, not being able to protect you."

"Don't worry about me, baby. Have you called your uncle?"

"I have. He's not doing so good. Peter has been over with him and says if I want to see him, I'd better do it soon. My last remaining family."

"Not true, sweetie, but I know how you feel. I just keep thinking of Melly. I feel in my bones that she's still alive, but what she's going through, I just can't imagine. She's tough, but whoever this psycho is..."

"I know, sweetheart. You have to do whatever you can to find your sister. Hero, I love you. I trust you. That the man's hands will be on you...Jesus, I want to kill him. But I trust you."

"I will never, ever betray that trust."

GEORGE HAD OBVIOUSLY DRESSED for a seduction. Hero tried to smile at him as he glided into the room. He reminded her of Al Pacino in Scarface. The effect was slightly comical, and Hero channeled her amusement into a welcoming smile.

"You look handsome."

He kissed her. "And you look ravishing." He ran his hand down the side of her slinky red dress; Hero tried desperately to not squirm away. "I have to admit, I've been thinking about this ever since you came to Como, Hero. The same as every man here."

Hero smiled and turned to get her purse. When she turned back, George was closer than she had realized, and he pulled her into his body. *God.* She could feel his erect cock against her belly, and her stomach flipped in disgust.

"Shall we go down to dinner?"

He smiled his snaky smile. "No, I changed the order. We're eating here."

A knock at the door and he opened it. Three waiters silently pushed three trollies into the room and then left just as quietly. Hero frowned. "Are you that hungry?"

George chuckled. "Just this trolley is our supper, dear one.

The rest...is for later."

Oh, dear God, what the hell is he playing at? Hero gave a nervous glance to the adjoining door; she hoped like hell Gaudio wouldn't miss his cue.

The food was, she had to admit, exquisite. A light dish of marinated salmon, a side salad, and crisp, flame-grilled asparagus. George poured white wine for them. Hero studied him. He really was the most arrogant man she had ever met. She knew he felt sure they would be having sex later.

Not happening, my friend.

The thought of him touching her made her want to throw up.

But she smiled and conversed politely, trying to get the measure of him. The more he spoke, the more she was convinced he was too damn stupid to have come up with everything her tormentor had put her through, and moreover, he was too vain to get himself into any bloodletting. He couldn't live the lifestyle he wanted from behind bars.

After dinner, Hero got up. "Shall we take our wine to the balcony?"

George smiled. "I don't think so, Hero. Come now. We both know why I'm here."

He got up and took her hand. "Come see the toys I have for us."

Toys? *Oh...shit.*

He lifted the silver platter covers to reveal a plethora of sex toys, lube, condoms...rope. "We can have a good time tonight, Hero. And just think of it...when I tell Arturo that I fucked his beautiful ex and the things she allowed me to do to her...you'll enjoy his pain, no doubt."

Hero tried to smile through the nausea. "Let me just go ... freshen up."

"Of course. Don't be too long."

Hero played along, sliding her finger under his tie and letting it slip across her hand. "Oh, I won't." *It'll only take a second to padlock my chastity belt.* Her nerves were making her want to giggle, and she fled to the bathroom, locking the door behind her. She snagged the burner phone from beneath the cabinet. "Gaudio...thirty-second warning."

"You got it."

Hero stuck the phone back and flushed the toilet, running the shower. She had put on sexy, but not transparent underwear, just in case things needed to get that far, but she couldn't bring herself to strip. She sucked in a deep breath...and went back out to see George, already shirtless, waiting for her. He held out his hand. "My dear..."

They both jumped as the fire alarm went off, screeching through the hotel. A look of pure frustration crossed George's face, and he reached for her again. "It's probably just a drill—"

Hero was already running toward the door. "I'm not taking that risk!"

Gaudio, I damn well love you.

She ran out, followed by a cursing George, tugging his shirt on. She made eye contact with Gaudio, who was helping people down the stairs and nodded, a tiny movement of her head. He winked at her.

Downstairs, the guests of the hotel were milling around in the evening air. It was cooler now, but Hero's adrenaline was racing. George wasn't letting her out of his sight. Once the alarm was found to be false, and they were allowed back into the hotel, he'd want her back to join him in his sordid little game.

Hero was quite aware of what he was doing. He wanted to brag to Arturo that he'd done things with Hero that Arturo never had—*wait.* Hero began to smile to herself. There was her answer right there. *Go big or go home.*

As she expected, they let them back in. Gaudio looked at

Hero, but she shook her head, mouthed, "It's okay. I got this from here."

BACK IN THE SUITE, Hero trailed her fingers over the dildos, riding crops, the paddles. She picked one up and studied it. George's eyes were alive with excitement. "Shall we?"

Hero put her best bored look on her face. "Is this it?"

That stumped him. "Sorry?"

She threw the paddle back on the trolley and looked up at him. "It's a little...tame for my tastes."

George rocked back a little. "Tame?"

Hero laughed. "Paddles, George? Riding crops? I outgrew them when I was fifteen." She sighed a bored, irritated sound and sat down. "What else you got?"

She had him. He had to save face in front of her. Hero prayed he wouldn't get nasty; she still had to be one hundred percent convinced he didn't know where Melly was, but as the minutes ticked by, she looked at the man in front of her and saw only a petty little toddler. George was no more a killer than she was.

George nodded. "I understand. I was testing your...taste for things. I thought, if I really told you what I like, you would get scared."

"What do you like, George?"

He smiled. "Maybe we should save this conversation for another night. The fire alarm killed the mood."

"It has." She stood and went to him, placing her hand flat against his chest. "Thank you for a lovely supper, George, but I think, for now I just want to focus on getting my sister back. After she's safe, well..."

George nodded. He pressed his lips to hers briefly. Hero broke away but smiled to soften the blow. "Goodnight, George."

"Good night, *bella* Hero."

CHAPTER TWENTY-TWO

She waited a good ten minutes after he'd gone to call Arturo. "Hey, gorgeous."

"Hey, *cara mia*. Listen, do me a favor. Double lock your hotel room door for me right now."

Hero's hackles went up, and she did what he asked.

"Now, close the drapes."

"Done."

Arturo gave a little laugh. "Now, come to the adjoining door to Gaudio's room."

She did and as she opened her side of the door, the other door opened, and she burst into laughter as Arturo came through the door, grinning at her.

"Gaudio called me…"

"How did you get in without being seen?" She threw her arms around him and kissed him until they were breathless.

"I have a friend with the *Vigili del Fuoco*, the fire service. They let me borrow a uniform, so when they were called to the false alarm…"

Hero laughed. "You're a genius. And I just so happen have a fire in me, Signore Fireman, and I need you to put it out."

Arturo grinned. "God, I missed you."

"Yeah, yeah, me, too. Fuck me, Bachi, right now."

Arturo swept her up into his arms and took her to bed. "I like this dress, Hero. I'm just sad he got to see it first."

"Rip it off me," she ordered. "I can get another red dress just for you."

Arturo did as she asked, tearing open the zipper and pulling the fabric off her. She was pulling at his sweater, yanking it over his head, desperate for him to be naked. Soon, their clothes were off, and Hero opened her arms to him. He hitched her legs over his shoulders and buried his tongue deep inside her, making her squeal.

"You must never spend another night away from me," he ordered, and she laughed.

"Keep doing that, and I won't want to, baby. *Oh, God, yes, that's it, right there...oh...*"

He went down on her until she was weeping with ecstasy and then drove his engorged and pulsating cock deep into her cunt, reaming it into submission as Hero writhed and moaned below him. His kisses were almost feral in his hunger for her.

"Hero," he panted, as they both approached their climax. "Marry me, for real, right now, tonight..."

Hero couldn't answer right away; her breath was taken away by the force of her orgasm, and she cried his name out again and again. Once they had collapsed back on the bed, she grinned at him. "The answer is yes, by the way, but I think we might have trouble finding someone to marry us at..." She glanced at the clock. "Three a.m."

"Watch me wake people up." He reached for the phone, but she stopped him.

"Don't. Tomorrow I'm going to Milan to meet with the consulate advisor. Come with me. We can do it there."

Arturo smiled, his delight obvious and real. "We're getting married."

"Yes, we are. For real." She kissed him, then sighed. "I have no right to be this happy when Melly is still missing."

"Hey," he stroked her face. "You deserve your happiness. Melly would want you to be happy. But we're not giving up on her, I swear to God. Did you get anything from Galiano?"

Hero shook her head. "Turo, there's something quite... pathetic...about him. It's like he's trying to prove to himself that he's better than you. I honestly think he hasn't got a clue about Melly or the threats against me. He simply hasn't got the darkness for this. He's spiteful and petty and an utter douchebag. But I don't think he's a killer."

"I hope you're right." Arturo shook his head. "God, that leaves Peter...but I can't bring myself to ask the questions."

Hero thought about it. "What if I ask? Not directly, of course, but...did you tell Peter about our ruse?"

"No, he thinks we've broken up, too."

"Gotcha. Then maybe I should reach out to him as your broken-hearted ex."

Arturo's mouth set in a line. "Putting yourself in the firing line again."

"Only if Peter...you know..."

She watched as a million emotions flitted through her lover's eyes. "Turo, for what it's worth, I can't imagine it's Peter. He just doesn't seem like the type, and why would he turn on you after all these years? For money, power? I don't buy it."

"Me either. He knows...God, he knows that if it was a choice between having you safe and alive or having the business, he could have it all. So why? Why would he do this?"

Hero nodded. "I agree. If he wanted me dead, he could have just done it quietly, and still gotten the same result. Why would he keep calling me and risk discovery? No, I don't buy it's Peter either."

They sat in silence for a long time, both lost in thought. Finally, Arturo turned to Hero and shrugged. "Then who?"

But she had no answer for him.

23

CHAPTER TWENTY-THREE

hen Hero woke in the morning, Arturo had gone. He'd left a note for her.

It's unlucky to see the bride before the wedding...also, we don't want Galiano to catch us.

Meet me at the City Hall in Milan at six p.m. A car is waiting to take you to the consulate and will bring you to the courtroom afterward.

I love you so much, Hero. See you at the end of the aisle.

A

xo

SHE SMILED TO HERSELF. After she'd showered and dressed, there was a knock at the door. A woman with a dress bag smiled at her. "Signore Bachi sent this over."

Hero thanked her and took the dress bag. Inside was the sweetest little white dress with another note.

. . .

FORGIVE MY PRESUMPTION. When all this is over, we'll do this again, and you'll have everything you ever dreamed about. But for now...this reminded me of you. A xo

THE DRESS WAS PERFECT—NOTHING over the top—just a light cotton dress that fell to just above her knees, a scoop neck, and sweet bell sleeves. It was perfect. Another two knocks on the door, and she had little white pumps with delicate beading and a thin gold chain which fell between her breasts. *He knows me in his bones,* Hero thought as she studied her reflection. *He knows me so well already.*

She felt vaguely tearful, and for a moment, scared. She grabbed her purse and pulled out her wallet, taking from it the photo of Beth and Tom. "I miss you both so much, but I'm going to be happy. I'm going to live the lives you should have had in your honor, my loves. I'll never, ever forget you. You are part of me."

She kissed the photo and traced the cheek of her lost daughter. "Sweet pea...maybe you'll have a brother or sister soon."

A few tears escaped then, and she quickly put the photo away. Another knock at the door, but when she opened it, her smile faded. "Oh."

George smiled at her. "And good morning to you, too. You look sensational."

Hero quickly recovered. "Dressing for summer. Hi, George, how are you?"

"Wondering if you'd like to spend the day together." He walked in without being asked, and Hero felt her body tense with irritation. She arranged her face into a friendly smile.

"I'd love to, but I have to go talk with the American Consulate in Milan. My car should be here in a while."

George waved his hand. "Cancel it. I can take you."

"No, thank you. They're used to seeing me with Arturo, and if I turn up with another man, they might think...well..."

"Ah, I see. They might suspect you flit from man to man and aren't a reliable witness?"

Hero's eyes narrowed. "That wasn't where I was going, but thank you, that's very comforting."

George wasn't in the least bit sorry for his slight. *Ah,* Hero thought, *still smarting from me outplaying him last night.* She sighed to herself. *Go away, little boy, I don't have time for your games.*

"Well, can I at least reserve some time for dinner tonight? Then perhaps we can continue the conversation we had last night."

"Not tonight, George. I'll call you. Now, I have to be going, so would you excuse me?"

His eyes narrowed, and for a second, Hero could see real rage flaring in them. As quickly as she saw it, it disappeared. "Of course," he said, smoothly. "I look forward to your call."

IN THE CAR TO MILAN, Hero tried to concentrate on what she would ask the man at the consulate, but soon, all she could think of was Melly. Where was she? Was she in pain? Was she hurt? Was she alive?

God. And here I am getting married without her. The guilt weighed heavy on Hero, but at the same time, she didn't want to wait a moment longer to be Arturo's wife. It felt like the safety harness she needed to get through all of this.

Besides all the hurt, the fear, and the terror, she had found something real, something shining amidst the rubble of her life.

The love of her life. Or rather, *another* love of her life. Hero couldn't weigh Tom and Arturo's love against each other—they were completely different, and she knew in her marrow that Arturo would honor Tom's love for Hero as he did his own. She wished with all her heart that they could have met. Would they have liked each other? She hoped so. Tom was so easy going and Arturo so charming.

Hero closed her eyes. *Sometimes, just sometimes, I wish life could be easy. That Arturo and I could be happy in our love without all of this pain, this hurt.* Without this psychopath targeting her for God knows what reason. *Whoever you are, just know, I'm not giving up. I get my happy ending this time, asshole, whether you wish it or not.*

Her resolve hardening, she opened her eyes and stared out at the beautiful countryside passing by for the rest of the journey.

DRIVING to the office he shared with Peter, Arturo made a decision. He would ask Peter outright if he wanted the business, and if Peter replied that he did, he would offer it to him. Give him everything he wanted. If the killer still pursued Hero after that... they were dealing with an unknown entity.

It would be a start. He would read his best friend and make a decision based on gut instinct whether Peter was lying or capable of hurting the woman Arturo loved. Or the women he loved and had loved. Peter had never liked Flavia much, but as a loyal (supposedly) friend to Arturo, he'd never expressed it to his face. But would he have murdered her? In such a personal, intimate way? If he wanted her dead, he could have easily arranged a hit and run or a random mugging. Flavia's killer wanted Arturo to know that he enjoyed killing her; that for him, it was an animal, sexual desire for her blood.

Arturo shook his head, trying to clear it of the images that plagued him. Flavia's body morphing into Hero's, bloodied and brutalized. *No. Not this time, motherfucker.*

He smiled at Marcella as he went into the office. "*Buongiorno*, Marcie. Is Peter in yet?"

"Sure is. Want some coffee?"

"Later, thanks."

Arturo walked down the hallway to Peter's office. His friend looked up and smiled. "Hey, I didn't expect to see you."

"Why not?"

"I thought you needed some time after the break-up. It seemed you took it pretty hard."

Arturo half-smiled. "I needed the distraction."

Peter nodded. "Fair point. Want to go over some numbers for the Patrizzi?"

"Not just yet. There's something else I wanted to talk to you about."

Peter looked interested. "Oh?"

Here goes.

"Pete…do you want my business? Or, rather, the family's business? Is it money you want or position?"

Peter was silent for a moment, his gaze searching Arturo's face for a reason behind his question. "Turo…"

"Just tell me. Do you want my business? If you do…it's yours. Just say the word. There are things more precious to me in this world than that."

Peter got up and went to close the office door. Sitting back down, he sighed. "Turo…what is this? Why are you asking me these questions?"

"I need to know…if you had a desire for more and what you would do for it."

"Such as?" Peter's voice had a hard edge now, but Arturo was in too deep.

"Would you...try and take the business from me by...dishonest methods?"

"The fuck, Turo?" Peter looked angry now, but Arturo pressed on.

"What I mean is...God, Peter...are you the person trying to kill the woman I love?" His voice broke at the end, knowing this conversation, at the very least, would most likely destroy his friendship with this man.

Peter dragged in a long breath. "You think I could kill Hero?"

"I don't know, that's why I'm asking."

"Jesus, Arturo. *Jesus H. Christ...*" He got up now and began to pace. "You really think I would...I take it this breakup is a ruse then?"

"Yes. We wanted to smoke Galiano out, but he's not picking up the bait."

"George is no killer, and just for the record, neither am I."

Arturo believed him. "I'm sorry. I had to ask, and I owed it to you, to be honest. You didn't answer my question about the business. Do you want it?"

Peter, his handsome face creased in anger and betrayal, leaned on the desk, blowing out his cheeks. "I don't want anything that would mean me murdering an innocent woman, Arturo. Do I want to move up in the business world? Of course. One day, I would like to be my own boss, but I'll do that *because* of your patronage, not despite it. Fuck, Arturo...you really think that little of me? After all these years?"

"No. But I had to know, I had to hear it from you," Arturo replied. "I'm sorry, Pete. Really. But Hero is everything to me. If I had to give up my business, every penny of my money to keep her safe, I would. I had to ask, my friend, because we're running out of ideas as to who is threatening her. Her sister is missing, and the police have no leads. Nothing. We are at our wit's end."

"I understand that." Peter's tone was softer now, understanding. He sat back down. "Look, I'm going to do everything I can to help you find this asshole, Turo, but looking at the people who you're closest to won't help here." He gave a wry smile. "Not even George. Do you really think he has the balls or the intelligence to pull this thing off?"

Arturo half-smiled. "No. I'm just desperate. He calls her, you know, the killer, and he tells her what he's going to do to her, how he's going to kill her. The most depraved stuff. She's so strong, Pete, but I'm scared he'll get to her."

"We won't let that happen. No psycho is going to kill her, Turo, I promise." Peter sighed. "We should go see your uncle. He has people at the highest echelons of government who might be able to help."

"We will...but not tonight. Tonight...Peter, I'm driving to Milan, and Hero and I are going to City Hall. We're going to get married. Officially. Legally."

Peter didn't argue for once, and Arturo went on, "It's just something we have to do for ourselves. Some kind of sanity in the midst of this craziness."

His old friend cracked a slight smile. "Marrying a woman you've known what, a month, maybe? Maybe that doesn't qualify as sanity..."

Arturo grinned. "Fair point. She makes me crazy in the best possible way. So, she and I will get married, and then we'll talk to my uncle tomorrow."

Peter nodded. "I'll call him and ask him to get his people onto Imelda's case tonight, and we'll go see him in the morning."

IN THE CAR on the way to Milan, Arturo thought about his conversation with Peter. He believed his friend when he said he would never hurt Hero...but there was still something niggling at the back of his mind. "What is it?" He murmured to himself as he parked the car outside the American Consulate.

His mind cleared though the instant he saw her walking down the steps to meet him. Hero's smile was wide, her eyes shining, and his heart began to beat out of his chest. Did she have something to tell him?

He got out and went to her. "What is it?"

Hero had tears in her eyes as she smiled at him. "It's Imelda. They've found her."

CHAPTER TWENTY-FOUR

"Run that by me again." Arturo was trying to make sense of what Hero was telling him as they drove to City Hall.

Imelda was safe...in Rome, Hero told him, and in fact, had never been abducted. On a whim, she had decided to take the train from Milan to Rome to spend a week or so 'off-grid.'

"She was really annoyed when she found out we'd all been looking for her. She said something to the effect of 'I'm a thirty-eight-year-old woman, and I can do what I like.' Apparently, the police who went to where she was staying were terrified of her."

"And she didn't think to call you?"

"She was pissed at me."

"Still."

Hero gave a soft laugh. "Who cares? She's *safe*. God, Turo, I feel a billion times lighter."

He took her hand. "It's fantastic news. So, we know your tormentor was bluffing now."

"But he knew she was missing, or at least that we thought she was missing. Which means..."

Arturo cursed. "It's someone close to us."

"Yup. Back to square one."

"Damn it."

Hero sighed. "Look, now that Imelda is safe, I feel a lot more confident in us getting to the bottom of this, and not only that, but now I can really enjoy this moment with you. We're getting married, Turo!"

Arturo looked at the woman he loved with all his heart and smiled. "You bet we are."

HERO CHANGED into her wedding dress in the bathroom at City Hall, brushing out her hair and reapplying some lip gloss. She loved the simplicity of this whole thing. It didn't matter if she didn't have a big meringue dress or a fancy reception party. The only thing that mattered was Arturo and their love.

They waited their turn, hand-in-hand. Arturo pressed his lips to hers. "You look beautiful, *cara mia*...and later, I'll show you just how beautiful."

Hero smiled. "I can't wait."

They were married in less than fifteen minutes and afterward, they kissed each other like it was their last time.

Hero finally broke away, laughing. "I need to breathe, hubby."

Arturo swept her up into his arms. "I had the foresight to book us a suite...I knew that after you became my wife, I wouldn't have the patience to drive us back to Como without having you first."

"You can have me all night long," Hero whispered in his ear. "For the rest of our lives. God, I love you so much, Arturo Bachi."

. . .

The white dress was on the floor seconds after they'd entered the suite, and now Arturo was caressing every part of her body, slowly, with obvious relish. He sucked on her nipples until they were rock-hard, then trailed his lips down to her belly, kissing the soft rise of it, rimming her navel with his tongue.

Then his mouth was on her sex as he lifted her thighs apart, hooking her knees over his shoulders. His tongue dipped deep into her cunt, tasting her honey, flicked around her clit until she was gasping and begging him to let her taste him, too.

He moved around so she could take his cock into her mouth and felt a warm rush of pleasure as her lips closed around him. The feeling of her tongue tracing around the sensitive tip of his cock was maddeningly exciting, her hands gently massaged his balls, then stroked his inner thighs as she hollowed out her cheeks to suck him. He came as he felt her tense, shooting into her mouth as she milked him, feeling her cunt tremble and contract with her own climax. God, she was beautiful, and yet he still couldn't believe she was his now—his entirely.

He moved around to kiss her mouth, stroking his hand down her body, feeling the lush curves of her, his hand coming to rest on her soft belly, splaying his long fingers out over it, imagining it rounded and swollen with his child.

Hero looked at him with shining eyes, and he knew she was feeling the same thing. "Shall we?"

Hero smiled, and as he moved his body on top of hers, her soft skin against his, she wrapped her legs around his waist and ground her damp sex against his burgeoning cock. "Fuck me, Turo...put your seed deep in me."

His cock was so hard and so heavy that it bobbed under its own weight against his belly, and when he notched it into the entrance of her cunt, he needed no help to thrust deep inside her. Feeling her vaginal muscles contract around it as he moved in and out of her, they both watched the movement, the way the thick length pulled in and out of her pink, swollen cunt.

"Look at us," he murmured, "we're beautiful."

Hero was breathless as they fucked, both of them entranced by the sight of their bodies moving together. When she came, she cried out his name, arching her back, her belly pressed against his as it trembled and undulated against him. Arturo groaned long and low as his cock shot the precious seed deep into her.

Finally, they collapsed together, laughing and panting for air. "I'll never get tired of this."

"Never."

They made love long into the night, ordering champagne at three a.m., which Arturo proceeded to spray all over her body. He licked every drop off of her, making her giggle and gasp with pleasure.

IT WAS four a.m. before they fell asleep, wrapped in each other. At five, Arturo got up to use the bathroom, reluctantly leaving the warmth of her arms. As he flushed the toilet and washed his hands, he heard something—a strange noise he couldn't place. He padded back into the bedroom and for a moment, stood, confused. Hero was in bed, the sheet pushed down past her hips. Laying on her back, she was breathing, but it wasn't natural breathing. She was gasping for air, gasping for...*oh, God, no*...his gaze drifted lower to where her hands were clasped over her belly...and blood bubbled up from between her fingers.

"*No, no, no...*" He dashed to her, lifting her hands to find her belly destroyed by stab wounds. This couldn't be happening...*no*...Hero looked at him, confusion and betrayal in her eyes.

"You didn't save me, you promised to save me..." Then she

gasped again, and her body jerked as if some invisible knife was being plunged into her again and again. Fresh wounds appeared in her soft belly...and he knew.

This isn't real...this isn't real...wake up. Wake up!

"Turo! Wake up! You're hurting me, *wake up!*"

Arturo opened his eyes to find himself on top of her, crushing her with his weight, his hands pressing down on her uninjured belly to stop the imaginary blood. He rolled off of her immediately. "God, I'm sorry, I'm sorry...are you okay?"

Hero was panting for air but nodded, her eyes large and frightened. "You were dreaming...then you just started to press down on me...I couldn't breathe."

He gathered her to him. "God, I'm so sorry, so sorry...I thought...I saw..." He couldn't say the words. Hero stroked his damp, dark curls away from his face, herself a lot calmer now.

"Was I dead?" Her voice was steady, and he nodded.

"You were dying," he amended, "and there was so much blood. I couldn't stop it. Couldn't stop it. *Mio Dio*..."

"Ssh, it's okay." She pressed her lips to his temple. "I'm perfectly fine; it was just a dream."

"A nightmare."

"A nightmare is all it was. Turo, Turo, Turo..." The way she whispered his name to comfort him was a balm on his frazzled nerves. He wrapped his arms around her.

"Hero, my love, my wife...we're going to make this right. I'm going to make this all go away."

She smiled at him, so lovely, the moonlight making her skin glow, her lips soft against his. "We're going to get through this, I swear we will. I love you."

"*Ti amo, il mia amore. Ti amo.*"

OUTSIDE OF THE HOTEL, he waited, the blacked-out windows of

his car making his surveillance easy. He knew what suite they were in—the penthouse. Arturo would settle for nothing less on his wedding night. So, they were married. It made no difference to his plan. Hero would be dead, and Arturo would be on his knees, utterly destroyed.

He wondered if they had any inkling that they had less than twenty-four hours left before they were ripped apart forever.

CHAPTER TWENTY-FIVE

"It's important that no one here or in Como knows you're safe and well in Rome," Arturo told Hero's adoptive sister the next morning. They were sitting in the American Consulate's meeting room on a conference call with Imelda, her lawyer, and the people from the Consulate. "If we can use the lie of your kidnapping to lure the killer out, all the better. He's going to use it, so we should, too. He'll try and force Hero to go to him to exchange for your safety—and we're going to let him think he's succeeded."

"That sounds dangerous to me," Imelda said sharply. "Hero, you're not going through with this, are you?"

"Of course I am, but I'll be perfectly safe. He thinks I'll be so damn worried about you that I will do whatever he says. Of course, I'll be wearing a wire and have a weapon of my own, and the police and Arturo will be there as soon as he takes me."

"I don't like this."

"Neither do I, Melly," Arturo said, "but it's the quickest, most efficient way to smoke him—or her—out."

"By using my baby sister as bait?"

Hero felt a rush of love towards Imelda. "Your baby sister?"

Imelda snorted, covering her slip. "You know what I mean."

"I love you, too," Hero said softly. "I would have died if anything had happened to you."

There was silence for a long moment. "Like I will if anything happens to you," Imelda said gently. "Please, Hero...there must be another way."

"I can't go on living like this," Hero said, "this is the quickest way. I promise you, Melly, I'm going to fight for this life. For my life."

There was a strangled sob at the end of the line, and Hero felt her eyes fill with tears. Arturo rubbed her back. "Melly," he said, his own voice breaking slightly. "I swear to you, in a few months, we'll all be together, and you'll be playing with your new nieces and nephews, and all of this will be over."

"You're not...?"

"Not yet." Hero chuckled softly. "Turo was just painting a picture."

Another silence. "I like that picture."

"We do, too. Now, the consulate is going to send over some people to protect you while this goes down. No, don't argue," Arturo told his sister-in-law, "it's just a precaution in case this psycho isn't working alone."

"Is that likely?"

"Anything goes."

"Christ. Just...promise me you'll stay alive, Hero. Make her promise, Turo."

"Oh, I have, and I will again. Over and over, Melly, I guarantee that."

AFTER THEY'D DISCONNECTED from Imelda, the Consulate people and the police went through everything again. Hero, wired and protected, would return to Como alone and pretend she was packing her things to leave. She would make her presence known every place she was connected with: the Patrizzi, Villa Charlotte, the art store, their favorite restaurants. She would carry the burner phone the killer called her on and answer his calls, telling him she was ready to exchange herself for Imelda.

And then they would wait. Arturo would return to Como separately, go through with his plan to visit his uncle with Peter. The police had agreed with Arturo—it was someone who knew them. "We'll have eyes on Galiano, the contractors at the Patrizzi, your friend at the art store...I'm sorry, but we really cannot trust anyone with your life except the people in this room. Even your uncle, I'm sorry to say."

Arturo nodded grimly. "I understand."

HERO AND ARTURO went back to their hotel to get their things before the separate cars picked them up. They held each other for a long time. "The worst part is waiting for him to make his move," Hero said. "If we could know this would all be over by the end of today, we could at least..."

"If you use the words 'say goodbye properly'..." Arturo closed his eyes, his face creasing with pain. Hero took his face in her hands.

"I wasn't going to say that. I was going to say 'we could start our married life properly.' Happily. It's going to be okay, I promise you that."

But they both knew she couldn't know that for sure.

"The cars will be here in an hour," Arturo stroked her face, "let's not waste a moment of this time now."

Just in case...

Their lovemaking was more intense that afternoon, as if they both recognized that it might be their last if all the planning went awry. As they moved together, Hero gazed at him and asked the question they both were thinking. "Do you think we have any idea what we're getting into?"

Arturo shook his head. "I'm not even sure I know what the hell is going on or even why this is happening. All I know is...I can't lose you."

"I feel the same."

He stopped moving for a second. "Promise me that if it comes to it, if things get crazy, you'll do everything or anything to stay alive. Promise me."

"I promise."

"Even if it means...offering yourself...God, I can't even..." Pain crossed Arturo's face as he faltered.

"I know." She nodded. "Anything goes. But I'll kill him before I let that happen."

Arturo winced again but nodded. "Do what you have to do, baby. I swear, we'll get through this."

He just hoped he was telling the truth.

THE CAR PULLED up outside the hotel in Como and dragging a deep breath into her lungs, Hero stepped out. To her relief, she got to her room without incident. Without her personal protection—her Gaudio—in the next room, she felt exposed and vulnerable.

She stripped off and went to shower, feeling the hot water easing her tense muscles. Dressing in jeans and T-shirt, she went into the living room to dry her hair.

"I hear congratulations are in order."

Hero whirled around with a gasp. George Galiano was sitting in one of the easy chairs. He smiled at her, but there was no warmth in it. He leaned forward. "*Signora* Bachi."

Hero's chin lifted. "What the hell do you think you're doing in here? How dare you invade my privacy like this?"

George smiled. "I have friends in this hotel. And everywhere in this town. Word travels fast. So, your little fake break-up was to what? Play me? Humiliate me?"

"Get out."

He moved too fast for her even to cry out. He slammed her against the window, one hand on her throat, one clamped over her mouth. Hero smelled liquor on his breath and saw the dangerous glint in his eye.

"I just came here to get what you owe me, Hero."

She bit his hand and he yelled, slapping her. "Go fuck yourself, George. I don't owe you a thing."

She pushed him away and darted around him, but he lunged for her, dragging her to the carpet and pushing up her shirt. He saw the wire immediately. "What the fuck is this?"

He yanked it off her, and Hero kicked out at him, catching him in the balls. Where the hell was her back up? Why weren't they busting down the door?

George grabbed her wrists as she struggled beneath him. "Stop fighting me, Hero, and this won't be unpleasant."

"You fucker…it was you? The whole time? Threatening my life?"

George snorted. "Why would I want to kill such a prime piece of ass like you, Hero? No, I just want to be buried deep in your perfect little cunt. Why should Bachi get all the ass around her? Now, I get to sample the goods."

His hand was burrowing down her jeans, and Hero began to panic. George grinned as he yanked her jeans down. "Relax, Hero…it'll all be over soon."

ARTURO CALLED out for his uncle as he pushed open the door to his uncle's mansion, but he heard nothing. He stopped. Something wasn't right here. Earlier, he'd called Gaudio and sent him over to protect his uncle if anything should go awry, and it wasn't like the bodyguard not to be at his post.

Arturo swallowed the feeling of panic and strode through to his uncle's study. Nothing. "Philipo?"

He checked the bedroom, the kitchen, and the living room. His uncle was nowhere to be found. Arturo yanked out his phone to call Hero, a nasty tightness in his chest.

Her phone went to voicemail. *Fuck...* Arturo turned to race to his car. He never saw the heavy marble bust before it smashed into his temple.

HERO WAS IN DEEP TROUBLE, and she knew it would take something extraordinary to get her out of this. George's entire weight was on top of her, one hand clamped over her mouth and nose, cutting off her air supply. Her head felt woozy, and she knew George would think nothing of killing her if she tried to resist. Instead, she went limp, faked passing out. She felt like screaming when she felt his cock, half-erect, nudge at her sex. *Please no, please not this, not like this...*

"I know you're faking, bitch," George's breath was hot against her cheek. "You better make this look good, or I will end you."

His hands slipped around her throat then and began to squeeze tighter and tighter. Hero choked, her eyes flying open as adrenaline coursed through her system. George grinned.

"Hello, pretty whore. Now, open those legs for me, and you might get to see tomorrow. You know I watched him put that knife in Flavia—God, it was the hottest thing I ever saw. I could gut you right here, Hero..."

Suddenly Hero got really mad, insanely raging, and with one mighty roar, she kicked him off of her. "*Motherfucker!* You want to kill me? Do it, you scumbag, do it now!"

She slammed into him as he tried to stand, his cock deflating, and knocked him against the plate glass window of the suite. It shuddered but stayed intact as George recovered himself. "Fucking little bitch...I'm going to rip you to pieces!"

He lunged for her just as the door to the suite was kicked in, and Peter Armley burst in, a gun in his hand. As George went for Hero, Peter shot him, the bullet slamming into George's forehead, splitting the back of his head wide open. George stopped dead, staring at Hero, then dropped to the floor, his eyes open and staring.

Hero, trembling so much she could barely stand, stared at Peter, at the gun in his hand. For a moment, she thought he might shoot her, but he shook himself, tucked the gun back into his waistband and grabbed a throw, wrapping it around her.

"Sweetheart, are you okay?" He hugged her to him, his voice gentle, and she couldn't help but be comforted by it. She shook her head.

"No...I'm not...not at all. Please, Peter, get me out of here. I need to be with Arturo."

Peter frowned. "Arturo? Do you know where he is? I've just been to his uncle's house. There's no one there. Even Philipo is gone."

Hero looked at Peter with horror in her eyes. "No...*no*...he went there...his car was maybe two minutes behind mine at the most...we have to go there."

She stood, wobbled and Peter caught her. "Sweetheart, we need to get you to the hospital..."

Hero's tears poured down her cheeks. "No, please, Peter, please..." She was sobbing then, barely able to get her words out. "We have to find him...George was working with someone... he told me he watched whoever it was killing Flavia. Please, Peter, we have to find Arturo before..."

"Okay, okay...okay...just, breathe for me, please. Take a deep breath, Hero..." He waited until she obeyed him and smiled. "Good. Now, can I help you get dressed?"

She shook her head and felt awkward as she pulled her jeans on as he watched. Her body ached from George's attack, but she pushed the horror of it to the back of her mind. There would be plenty of time to break down later when they were all safe.

Peter locked the hotel suite door behind them. "We'll explain about George's body later."

As they hurried to the elevator, Hero wondered again where the hell her protection was, why the plan had gone so badly wrong.

As Peter helped her into his car, Hero searched the street for any sign of the police. Nothing. What the hell was going on?

"Here." Peter handed her a hip flask. "It's just Scotch, but it might make you feel better."

Hero hesitated, but as Peter started the car and turned to drive out of town, she took a sip, then a large swig. He was right; it did feel better.

"Peter?"

"Yes, sweetheart?"

Hero swallowed. "Do you think Arturo is..." She couldn't bring herself to say the word 'alive.'

Peter reached over and took her hand. "It's going to be okay, darling. I swear it is."

She squeezed his hand. "Thank you for saving me, Pete. George was going to kill me."

His fingers tightened on hers. "No, baby, he wasn't. George couldn't kill anyone. He didn't have the balls. What he did to you...that was the limit of his vileness. I'm so sorry that happened."

"Thank you." Her throat felt tight, but the alcohol had

flooded her system it seemed, and she began to feel lightheaded. *Too* lightheaded. "I don't feel right."

"It's the shock, honey. Are you sure I can't take you to the hospital? You might need it."

"No. Arturo...I need to get to him..." Her voice sounded distant to her, and her ears rang suddenly. "What's happening to me?"

"I told you. Shock."

She swallowed. "Did Arturo call you? He wanted you to meet him at Philipo's?"

Peter laughed, but it was curiously mirthless. "I told you that, too. He called me, told me he'd found your sister, asked me to come get her to bring her to you. When I couldn't find him at Philipo's, I went to Villa Claudia. Your sister was there. She told me to come find you at the hotel. That's how I knew to find you there."

It was like an icicle being shoved into her heart, and instantly, Hero knew their worst fears were confirmed. She turned to look at him as he glanced at her, smiling, but his eyes were cold and dead.

"Oh my God," she whispered and lunged for the steering wheel. Peter laughed as she struggled with him, then slammed his fist into her temple. The blow was so hard, her head bounced off the side window. Hero moaned from the blow, struggling to take her seat belt off, clawing at the door of the car. Peter laughed.

"Don't bother, beautiful, besides I'm doing what you asked. I'm taking you to Arturo."

Hero, feeling her consciousness begin to slip, stared at him in horror. "Did you kill him?"

"No. I didn't kill Arturo, but like you, he may wake up with a little headache. By the way, if you're feeling a little woozy, it's because of the drug that's in the Scotch. I thought you might get a little feisty."

"What happened to the polizia?" Her voice was getting faint. "Why didn't they come?"

"Never underestimate the power of money, Hero."

She was fighting the sedative. "You want his money."

"No, you stupid bitch...I want *him*. How come neither of you, you or Flavia, neither of you could see...Arturo belongs to *me*."

Hero looked at him and saw the depth of his obsession. Peter was in love with Arturo? "You love him."

"I'm not gay," he said, sharply. "It goes beyond sexual love, but I don't expect you to understand that. You and Flavia...there are a lot of differences, but the one thing you have in common is that you see his physical beauty, his kind heart, but you don't see *him*."

"You're lying...I *do* see him. I see every part of him..." Her voice trailed away, and her vision faded for a moment...then... "You killed Flavia."

"Yes."

"And you're going to kill me?"

"Yes, Hero. I'm going to kill you. Only this time, I'm going to make Arturo watch as I stab you to death. He'll watch the light go out in your pretty eyes and know it was all for nothing. That he again tried to love someone other than me, and it ended the same way as it always will. I'm going to enjoy killing you, Hero."

"You're insane..." The darkness was approaching relentlessly now. Peter reached over and stroked a finger down her cheek.

"And you're about to be just another dead whore, Hero... sleep now. Don't worry. I'll make sure you're awake to feel my knife driving into you."

Hero fought unconsciousness, knowing it was her only chance, but then it overwhelmed her, and she sank beneath it, knowing she might never wake up again.

. . .

Peter pulled up in front of Philipo's villa, and for a moment, he smiled as he studied Hero's inert form. "You really are very lovely," he said, and pushed her T-shirt up, exposing her belly. He splayed his fingers over it, stroking the gentle curve of it, imagining how the skin would split under his knife. "Yes, you are perfect. I understand why he loves you. But for you, his love is a death sentence. A shame...I actually like you very much."

He got out of the car and went around to the passenger side, lifting her out easily. He carried her into the villa, going straight to the kitchen. He laid her on the table in the kitchen. "This will have to suffice as my sacrificial altar, sweetheart."

He left her, unconscious, and yanked open the door to the basement. In seconds, he was hauling a semi-conscious Arturo up the stairs. "Come on, Turo."

He dumped Arturo into a chair and watched as his friend, his great love, focused on Hero's unconscious body. Peter smiled then. "It's time to say goodbye, Turo."

And he raised his knife.

CHAPTER TWENTY-SIX

Arturo threw himself towards Peter just as Hero opened her eyes and saw the knife curving down towards her. Her self-preservation instincts kicked in and she rolled her legs up and kicked the knife away, just as Arturo tackled Peter.

Both men tumbled to the floor, grappling with each other. Peter began yelling as Hero rolled off the table. "Don't fucking move, bitch. This is when you die."

"Fuck you, psycho." Hero scooted around to help Arturo. His beautiful face was soaked in blood from the vicious wound on his head, and for a moment, Hero felt herself freeze with distress.

"Go! Run!" Her lover screamed at her as he tried to quell Peter's attempts to get to her but Hero, adrenaline beginning to course through her veins, smiled grimly.

"Not a fucking chance. This is where it ends for you, Peter."

Peter laughed at her and then struck Arturo directly on his head wound, knocking him to the ground once more. Arturo couldn't help releasing his grip as he groaned in agony, and Peter took off after Hero, who ran to the other side of the kitchen, grabbing anything she could get her hands on to fight him with.

Peter, tall and broad, dwarfed her, easily knocking the pans and weapons from her. Hero kicked out, aiming for his balls but he grabbed her foot and twisted it until she lost balance.

He grabbed her, hauling her struggling body to where Arturo was trying to get to his feet again. Hero bucked and jerked, kicking backward as Peter kept his grip on her.

"Turo," he growled, his mouth spraying saliva onto Hero's face as he held her near. "Time to watch her die."

"No!" Arturo clambered to his feet, barely able to stand now as Peter laughed. For a moment, time froze as Hero and Arturo stared at each other in desperation, then Arturo lurched towards them as Peter sunk his knife deep into Hero's stomach. She didn't even cry out—the breath from her lungs was pushed out as the blade sunk into her. *No. No.* This wasn't going to happen. It didn't end this way. Arturo's beautiful, bloodied face was a mask of utter horror.

Despite her agony, Hero stamped on Peter's toes as hard as she could muster, and he yelped in surprise, obviously expecting her to be laid low by the stabbing. His grip released slightly, just enough for her to slip from his reach. Then Arturo was on him, knocking Peter down. Hero stamped again, on Peter's wrist this time, and he released the knife.

She scooped it from the floor, but her body was shutting down from the blood loss. She clutched at the wound with one hand, and lurched towards the fighting men, knife in hand.

As Hero reached them, Peter made the mistake of looking around at her. Arturo slammed his hand under Peter's jaw, causing him to bite through his own tongue. In an agonized rage, Peter jerked back...and Hero drove the knife into his throat.

Peter stared at her in shock, blood gushing from his wound.

Then one last breath seeped out of him, and he slumped to the floor, eyes staring.

ARTURO KICKED his body out of the way and went to Hero. She was coughing up blood, and he took her in his arms, barely conscious himself.

"No, please, hold on, *cara mia*...someone will come... someone will come..."

Hero gazed up at her husband and smiled. "I love you so much, Arturo Bachi. So, so much."

Arturo's tears were pouring down his cheeks, mixing with the blood. "This isn't the way this ends."

"Just...hold me until the end. Please." Her voice was fading now, and her eyes closed.

"Hero...Hero....no, wake up, wake up..."

But she wouldn't wake up, and Arturo knew it was over. He cradled her in his arms and closed his own eyes, praying that death would come for him soon.

Darkness fell...

VOICES. Familiar and not-so-familiar. *Help us. Help her...please...*

"Turo...Turo? Open your eyes, son."

Arturo opened his eyes to a bright, white room which made his vision scream with pain.

"That's it, Turo. Good. You're in the hospital, son." He knew that voice. Philipo.

"Uncle?"

A rough-skinned hand took his. "It's me. You've been unconscious for a week now. They had to operate. You had a brain bleed, son."

Arturo didn't care. "Hero..." *Please don't say she's dead, please, please...*

"Baby?"

Her voice made all the breath leave his body. "Hero?" Finally, his eyes focused as his love, the one true love of his life, leaned over him and kissed his parched lips.

"I'm here, baby. I'm not going anywhere." She was pale, her dark hair in a messy ponytail, but she had never looked more beautiful.

"Are you okay? You were stabbed! I thought..."

"I was lucky; the knife missed my major arteries and organs."

Philipo put his arm around Hero. "She's lived up to her name, Turo. She crawled out of my kitchen to your car, found your cell phone, and called the police."

Arturo, his hand seeking hers, squeezed it tightly. "I thought you were dead. You...there was so much blood."

Hero nodded. "When I woke up, you were so deeply out, I knew I had to get help for us." She smiled a little ruefully. "It took me a while. I kept passing out, but eventually, I got there."

"You're up and walking." Arturo shook his head in amazement, then winced at the pain.

"You know me," she said, smoothing his hair away from his face, smiling down at him. "Ain't nuthin' gonna keep me down."

"*Mio Dio*, I love you, Hero Donati."

She smiled. "Hero *Bachi*," she said gently, and he grinned.

Philipo cleared his throat. "Ah, yes. I have something to say about that. You got married and didn't invite me?"

Hero hugged the old man. "Don't worry, when we're both healed, we'll have a big old meringue-fest at the *Villa Claudia*. My parents are here, too," she told Arturo, then grimaced as Melly stepped into the room behind her. "And so is Melly. She makes sure I don't exert myself too much." Hero rolled her eyes.

Arturo chuckled softly. "I can't wait to meet your parents."

Hero bent down and kissed him, and now he noticed that she moved gingerly, still recovering from her wounds. "*Ti amo.*"

"*Ti amo*, Hero. Listen...what happened to...?"

"The police are handling everything. It has turned into a little bit of an international incident. The Consulate is not happy with the Italian polizia, it's safe to say. They're still trying to figure out how Peter got his information and how he managed to get us into that situation."

"He's dead?"

Hero's sweet face hardened. "Stone cold. Good riddance."

"He killed Flavia?"

She nodded.

Arturo was amazed to see Imelda wrap her arms around Hero without any hesitation and hold her fiercely. "If Armley hadn't killed George, I would have done it myself, for trying to force himself on my baby sister."

Arturo blanched. "Did he—Hero—I—"

"No. Very close. But no." She shook her head and leaned into her sister's embrace.

Arturo sighed in relief, and Imelda reached out her free hand and took Arturo's.

"So much damage, but we're on the other side of it now. I will do everything in my power to make sure you're both okay."

Philipo twinkled at her. "I might be a little bit in love with you, Imelda Donati."

Imelda grinned at him. "Right back at you, handsome."

For a moment, Hero and Arturo looked at each other and grinned, and Imelda released her sister. "Come on, Phil, let's go grab some coffee and leave these two alone for a while."

Alone, Arturo patted the bed. "I'll shift over...I need to hold you in my arms."

Somewhat awkwardly, they managed to curl up in his hospital bed together. Hero nuzzled her face into the crook of his neck, kissing along his jawline. Arturo stroked his hand down to her abdomen, feeling the heavy dressings there. "Does it hurt?"

"The muscles do when I move, but they'll heal. It's not so bad, really. I got lucky."

Arturo gave a mirthless laugh. "Lucky? I let him hurt you."

"You did nothing of the sort. I would be dead right now if it weren't for you."

They were both silent for a moment, recalling the horror of that day. "Seeing you on that table like some sacrificial lamb...*mio Dio*, Hero. I thought that was it. I didn't know if I had the strength to fight him off, but there was no way I was going to let him..."

"...gut me like a pig. What he did to Flavia. He was in love with you, Arturo. He swore up and down he wasn't gay, that his love transcended gender, that you had always belonged to him."

Arturo winced. "What the fuck?"

"He was crazier than a soup sandwich."

Arturo, despite the topic, had to laugh. "A what?"

"Just a saying."

"A Chicago saying?"

Hero grinned. "No, I heard it on a television show one time. But it's true."

Holding her in his arms again felt so right, so blissful, that he forgot his pain. "Hero, when we both get out of here, we're going to begin our life together all over again."

Hero smiled at him. "You bet we are, gorgeous..."

And she kissed him so passionately that he forgot anything else in the world existed apart from the two of them.

CHAPTER TWENTY-SEVEN

Six months later...

HERO GIGGLED as Arturo stole the towel that was wrapped around her body. "Turo, we're going to be late."

"I don't care...you look so adorable all wet and sexy." He pulled her onto the bed where he waited for her, and she sighed happily as his lips met hers. She could feel his long, thick cock pressing against her bare belly. She wrapped her legs around him.

"You're intoxicating, Signore Bachi." She gave a long moan as he slid inside her and began to move. Arturo smiled down at her as they made love, his arms locked either side of her head.

She stroked his face as he plunged his cock in and out of her. "God, I love you."

Arturo chuckled. "*Ti amo, il mia amore...per sempre...*" Forever...

She smiled up at him. "Fuck me hard, Bachi, until I can't walk straight."

"My pleasure." He pinned her hands to the bed and began to thrust hard, Hero tilting her hips up to take him inside her as deep as she could.

"We are definitely going to be late...*oh...oh yes...God... Turo...yes!*"

STILL GLOWING FROM THEIR LOVEMAKING, Hero took the hand Arturo offered her and got out of the car. The piazza in front of the newly renovated Villa Patrizzi was full of press and partygoers for the grand opening. The hotel's signage was covered with a tarpaulin, no doubt so Arturo—or rather the invited dignitary—could unveil it as part of the ceremony.

Arturo and Hero mingled with the crowds, seeing their friends waiting to greet them. Gaudio had been given the night off, and he greeted them as old friends with Fliss wrapped in his arms. Hero grinned at her. "Still going strong?"

"You bet it is. I'm moving in with him next week."

Hero hugged her. "I'm so happy for both of you. Let's get together soon, yes?"

"Definitely. Oh, looks like your man is about to give his speech."

Arturo was indeed on the stage with the invited guest, an international movie star who had a villa on the Lake. Arturo introduced his guest, and the actor made a brief speech, but then quickly turned back to Arturo.

"Now, you might think I'm here to pull the cord and unveil the hotel's sign...but in this case, friend, considering the circumstances, I think that honor should fall to you. So, without further ado, please give it up for my good friend and the genius behind this place, Arturo Bachi."

Hero applauded wildly with the crowd, knowing Arturo would be a little taken aback by this.

Arturo stepped back up to the microphone, thanking his guest. Then he paused for a moment, seeming to take a breath in. "Friends...it's not a secret what I had long planned for this place, and the...how should I say...*checkered history* I have had with it. Last year, I almost had all the pieces in place...then a beautiful stranger came in and changed everything. My whole life. And, *mio Dio*, I'm so very thankful that she did. Hero Donati...you are my love, my life, my wife, and this place would mean nothing if it weren't for you.

"This hotel has been years in the making, but to me, it only became a reality when Hero entered my life. So, when it came to renaming this place, there was no competition. Without further ado, ladies and gentlemen, I welcome you to the *Villa Hero*."

Hero gasped in shock, and a million flashbulbs went off as Arturo pulled the cord, the tarp slipped to the ground, and the huge, wrought iron sign lit up. *Villa Hero.*

There were tears in her eyes, and she fought her way through to him. "I can't believe it, thank you...God, what an honor, Turo." She felt giddy and discombobulated as the crowd jostled them, but when Arturo took her in his arms, everything melted away.

"The honor is all mine, Hero Donati Bachi, it always was..." And he kissed her until her senses swirled, and the noise of the crowd became nothing more than a song on the morning breeze.

THE END.

SIGN UP TO RECEIVE FREE BOOKS

Sign Up to Receive Free E-Books and Audiobook Codes.

Would you like to read **The Unexpected Nanny, Dirty Little Virgin** and **other romance books for free?**

You can sign up to receive these free e-books and audiobooks by typing this link into your browser:

https://www.steamyromance.info/free-books-and-audiobooks-hot-and-steamy/

Or this one:

https://www.steamyromance.info/the-unexpected-nanny-free/

PREVIEW OF DR. ORGASM

A VIRGIN AND A BILLIONAIRE ROMANCE

By Scarlett King
& Michelle Love

Blurb

Maddy:

It's amazing what you can do when you don't care if you live or die. Like escape from the hellhole where you have been a prisoner for half your life. Or ride off on the back of a hot stranger's motorcycle. Aaron is the first guy I have ever met that I have felt this way about. I like him. I trust him. I want him. But if I follow his lead and start wanting to live again, what happens when someone tries to drag me back into the hell I escaped from?

Aaron:

I'm falling for a mystery girl that I just talked out of jumping off a bridge. I shouldn't let myself. She needs help, support, maybe even protection—not sex. But as I try to show her that life is worth living, nature starts taking its course. Soon enough the best lessons I can teach her are the ones between the sheets ... and she is more than willing. But I'm about to stumble across an ugly truth about my Maddy that will make me rethink everything—and will put us both in danger.

CHAPTER 1

Aaron

It's almost midnight by the time I drive my motorcycle out of Ravenwood Hospital's sprawling parking lot. It's a foggy night, turning the road into a tunnel and the surrounding forest into something ghostly and surreal. It's the perfect weather for Halloween.

I love Halloween—I've been a horror movie buff since I was ten. I grew up on a ranch twenty miles from town in Wyoming, so the thirty-first of October meant a special dinner, pumpkin lanterns, and a lengthy horror movie marathon instead of trick or treating. I loved those nights.

I'm dead tired and I don't much mind that I won't be home in time for any Halloween parties. Behind my visor, my eyes are bleary from checking and rechecking dozens of forms. It was back-paperwork night in the cardiology wing, and as the youngest director in Ravenwood's hundred-year history, I didn't have any excuse to leave early.

I had two assistants helping me out—Becky, a veteran of the department, and Kate, who is less experienced but a harder worker. I needed both to help me plow through this month's paperwork, which included the annual financial report and an assortment of federal grant applications. Now, each and every last scrap of paper has been filed, recycled, or followed up on, and I'm fleeing back to my mansion before more comes in.

My head stings, my back aches, and I'm dehydrated. I know that enough fluids, a good meal, and a visit to my home gym and jacuzzi will fix everything. Meanwhile, though, I have to get home down a winding coastal road, with wet streets and swirling wind to deal with. Good thing I'm steady under pressure.

At least the rain has let up. The wet branches drip on me as I drive out onto the main road, humming Metallica's "Enter Sandman" under my breath.

Ravenwood sits in the wooded hills just outside Marin County, in one of the most beautiful regions in California. The air is clean here, there's plenty of rain and open land, and the sea goes on forever outside the Golden Gate. The area is at its best in high summer, with warm, slightly misty nights full of stars.

In fall, however, it's ... well, I find it perfect, but some of my coworkers find it creepy as hell. Especially since we have to cross a gorge on our way off hospital grounds, and the spooky looking bridge we have to use is always dark, falling under the shadow of towering trees with no lights to guide the way. At night, you have to use your high beams and pray there are no surprises waiting for you.

I'm trying to sort out what movies to watch as I approach the stretch of road that leads to the bridge. The road is just wide enough that I can see the moon through the break in the trees, sailing ahead of me high and silver, with a pattern that always reminds me of watermarks.

"John Carpenter?" I muse aloud. Classic horror is always

good. Problem is I already did a John Carpenter marathon a few months ago. Though I love his creepy stuff, I need a palate cleanser.

"Huh," I mutter. I have a bad habit of talking to myself when alone.

"*Tales from the Crypt*? Something from the *MST3K* collection?" Nah, too campy. I frown as I go around a turn. I can see the faint shape of the bridge looming half a mile up the road.

"J-horror?" The Japanese have their own very distinct style of horror, and some of the best people in the business these days come from there. I've been working my way through the *Ring* series which, except for the crack-fest of the second movie, has managed to be both poignant and terrifying. I haven't seen the prequel about Sadako, *Ringu o*, and decide to put it on first when I get home.

There's nothing like a Japanese ghost story. Figures in white, with streaming black hair, transformed from demure wives, mothers, and daughters to betrayed, rage-filled entities whose power seems bottomless. The fact that these horrible monsters are often played by fetchingly pretty actresses only adds another layer of creepiness to it all.

I nod to myself, satisfied. That's one movie down to watch while I have my steak and beer. The household staff will be gone for the night except for my security team, but I'm sure I can sort out reheating my dinner.

Too bad I have no date to share movie night with. Being a department head in my mid-thirties tends to eat up all my free time. And a relationship requires a lot more than a quick date or fuck during my few spare hours on weekends.

At least now, with the backlog of paperwork, phone calls, and meetings eliminated, I can think about going out to a bar or something this coming weekend. It's been a while since I even danced with a woman, let alone took one to my bed. I miss it, in that bone-deep way that leads to dirty dreams and the occasional reckless decision.

I'm almost at the bridge. My Harley's headlights splash across the weathered wood and I peer ahead, catching sight of something emerging out of the fog. "What the hell is that?" I mutter.

There is something white standing in a misty patch of moonlight about halfway across the bridge. It's human-sized, if smaller than me—though almost everyone is. It has either black hair or a black shawl hanging over its shoulders, and it's dressed in flowing white—either a robe or a coat.

For a moment, my tired brain goes *oh shit oh shit oh shit* and I'm certain that either this is a nightmare or reality just took a hard left. But a split second later I get hold of myself and let out a laugh as I slow down.

"Oh, man, no way." I'm not looking at a Japanese ghost. I'm looking at a young, living woman who just really looks the part.

I slow down enough to have a better look and to give her a compliment on her costume. Not a catcall. That's not my style. But she did just scare the crap out of me—mission accomplished as far as dressing like Sadako.

As I slow the bike down she squints up at me, holding up one slim, pale hand to shade her eyes. She's not Japanese, though her petite build and straight, silky black hair make me think she could be mixed. Her wide, deep brown eyes catch my attention then, and I find myself falling into them before I can stop myself.

"Uh ..." I manage as I stop and turn the headlight away from her, just enough to keep the glare out of her face. "Hi! Nice costume."

"Costume?" She looks down at herself, and I get a better look at her as I wonder if she's a bit high. She's actually wrapped in a lab coat that is about five sizes too big for her, making it float around her dramatically in the wind. Beneath it, I catch sight of an overlarge pale sweater and the silvery drape of a velvet skirt. It's all too big for her, but she's so waiflike that it almost looks like a deliberate fashion choice. If not, as I thought before, a costume.

"I'm sorry, are you okay?" I ask suddenly. I've seen people with this shocked, sad look on their faces before—usually when I'm talking to the family of someone we lost on the table. It doesn't happen too often, but that haunted expression sticks with you. So I notice it right away.

She stares at me as if she has no idea what to say. The wind picks up, hissing through the pine branches and sending her hair and clothes drifting around her. We watch each other mutely. After a pregnant pause she lifts her head and gives me the saddest smile I have ever seen in my life.

"No," she replies simply, and my heart sinks.

CHAPTER 2

Madelyne

The sky is so enormous, now that I am free. I have been indoors for so long that I feel dizzy as I stare up at the slowly disintegrating clouds, as if I will be overwhelmed if I don't look away. And it's not just the sky; the whole world outside the asylum is vast.

I MANAGED to avoid swallowing some of my meds before bed check, spitting them out and flushing them instead. It's been a good two hours since then—just enough time to slip out and steal clothes from the nurses' lockers and to hike this far down the road. Problem is, the pills still partially dissolved in my mouth before I could get rid of them, so I'm lightheaded as I turn to the man on the motorcycle.

. . .

I DIDN'T EXPECT anyone to be out driving this late in the middle of nowhere. The fact that he came from the direction of the hospital makes me a little nervous. But Ravenwood is huge—the campus has three separate complexes on it, including the mental hospital.

It's possible that he doesn't even work in the same building. I try to remind myself of that fact as he dismounts from the bike and pulls off his helmet. When I see his face, everything else leaves my mind for a few moments.

I DON'T KNOW anything about men or attraction. I haven't had the opportunity to do anything but admire boys from afar. But suddenly my stomach flutters, I feel a warm flush in my cheeks, and the dark thoughts that have been swirling through my head part like clouds before the moon.

HIS HAIR IS a sort of tawny brown color, like a lion's mane—shot with gold threads that reflect the glow from the motorcycle headlights in sparks. It stands up from a high forehead, mussed by his helmet. The lean, tanned face beneath is prickled with blond stubble along his jawline. His mouth is generous and well-shaped, and his narrow green eyes stare into mine like he's looking right through me.

HE'S ALSO HUGE, I realize as he dismounts his motorcycle and stands up straight. He looms over me, and only his gentle expression keeps me from freaking out and putting more space between us.

"What's your name?" he asks me softly.

. . .

I blink at him, reluctant to tell him. He could hear, later, about a missing patient named Madelyne at this very hospital. But then I just shake my head slightly, amused with myself. Unless he's a regular visitor to the hospital, he's not likely to hear anything. I doubt they'd let my name get out to the public. "Madelyne."

"That's a pretty name. I'm Aaron. Do you need some kind of help?" He tilts his head slightly, and I shrink a little under his piercing gaze. He's intimidating without even meaning to be, even when he's being kind.

"I … no. There's … not much that can be done, really. I'm just going to … spend a little time around here, that's all." I struggle to sound casual and wonder why it's so hard for me to keep the shaking out of my voice suddenly. "You can … you can go on. I'll be okay. Really."

The gorge is deep and shadowy, with rocks like jutting fangs. I can hear rushing water down there. The whole idea of throwing myself over the railing terrifies me.

But if there's one thing I know, it's that they will catch me if I stay on the run. I have no family, no friends, no money, nowhere to go. It doesn't matter that I don't have any of the illnesses that I was hospitalized for, except, of course, for the depression. The doctor will not let me be free as long as I am alive.

Aaron gives a deep, resigned sigh, and before I know what he's doing he leans against the weathered railing, not so inconspicuously placing himself between me and the brink. He folds his powerful arms and the leather of his jacket creaks against his biceps.

"I don't think you're going to be okay if I leave you, sweetheart," he says in a calm tone that leaves me with tears brimming in my eyes. "As a matter of fact, I think that if I leave you here, they'll be pulling you out of the gorge tomorrow morning."

"Oh, that's nonsense. I—" I start, then realize that I have started fidgeting. "I'm ... I just ..."

"Look," Aaron says softly, catching my eye. "I don't know what's brought you out here like this. I don't know what you're going through, and I'm not gonna judge. But I am gonna ask you something."

I stop fidgeting and lick my lips, gathering my wits. How did he know what I was planning? I wipe my eyes impatiently. "What?"

"If you don't care whether you live or die anyway, then how about you come take a ride with me instead?" His smile is charming, his tone reasonable. But his eyes bore into mine, seeking my answer.

. . .

This wasn't in my plan. Confusion swamps me again and I stand still, blinking back at him. "Why would you do that?" I ask.

He shrugs. "I can't just leave you. But I can't tell you what to do with your life either. If you don't mind my saying so, you look a little ambivalent about the whole ... situation here. I figure maybe a nice ride will help you clear your head."

I hesitate. It's true that I have nothing left to lose. It's true that if anything, taking this man up on his offer gives me a chance at a running start before the doctor finds out I'm missing.

Escaping with my life might be possible after all. Or if it isn't, maybe I can just have a little fun before I go back to my first option.

I walk over to the motorcycle, which gleams black and silver in the moonlight. It's huge and powerful-looking, like its owner. Maybe he's a biker that was discharged from the emergency wing. Maybe he's not the type to turn me in.

Nothing to lose but my life, and I was an inch from giving that up anyway.

I look back at him and nod. "Let's go."

CHAPTER 3

Aaron

"I've never ridden a motorcycle," she confesses, and I smile and pull my spare helmet from my saddlebag.

I'm so relieved that she agreed to my plan to keep her from killing herself that it feels like a weight has lifted off my chest. I came up with it by the seat of my pants.

But I became a doctor for a reason: to save lives. I wasn't about to just leave her there.

"Here. I'll get on, and you climb on after me. I'll show you where to put your feet." I look her over. "Do you have anything to put your hair up with?"

She didn't, so I take a strip of gauze from my saddlebag's emergency kit and tie her hair in a low ponytail. "Here you go."

Mom and Dad have never understood why I would leave their land in Wyoming, which expands every year and is full of every possible luxury or bit of wilderness that a man could possibly need. But I wanted to make my own mark. It wasn't enough for me to simply inherit Father's pharmaceutical company—or the ranch built by its wealth—and coast on his achievements.

So med school it was. And then my specialty, and then my residency. I started climbing the ladder at Ravenwood in my late twenties, when most people my age were still finishing grad school. I was far too focused on my goal to let myself waste time.

My attention is brought back to Madelyn as she adjusts her ponytail. She's skittish, shifting nervously when I touch her. I don't feel too bad about that. I don't know what hell she has been through, but as long as she isn't jumping off a fucking bridge I figure she's better off for my intervention. I just know I can't expect her to treat me like a hero because of it.

I help her get the helmet on, wrap her in my leather jacket, and get on the bike. After a few moments of hesitation, she gets on behind me. I feel her arms slip around my chest under my arms, and feel an unexpected jolt of pleasure.

. . .

Shit. This woman is distraught enough to be contemplating suicide. I can't even think about my attraction to her until she's stable. I absolutely have to make certain that she's okay first.

First, do no harm, I think as I rev the engine. "Okay. Hold onto me firmly, and if you get scared, let me know."

She buries the front of her helmet in my back as we take off down the road. Her arms squeeze me tight—she's already scared. But she doesn't stiffen up and she doesn't tell me to stop, so I keep going.

There's a possibility that she's playing me and will jump off the damn bike as soon as we get up to speed. I don't know what I'll do if she does that, besides get an ambulance here as fast as I can.

In a way, we're both forced to have faith in each other. As we leave the bridge behind and drive off into the dark, I can feel her relax just a little, and continue to do so bit by bit as we get closer to the coastal highway. We can't talk, and besides monitoring her and the road, I'm pretty much left to my thoughts.

I was made head of Ravenwood Hospital's Cardiology Department early last year after the old head, Dr. Emil Blanchley, retired abruptly after breaking the nose of the head of the psychiatric wing. I can't say that I blame him one bit for landing that punch—Dr. Westridge is a prick. But rules are rules, and while some members of the board chuckled about it, Blanchley was told to retire immediately if he wished to keep his pension.

I'VE BEEN SCRAMBLING to clean up after him ever since, going through years of neglected paperwork that has demanded many late nights. Blanchley might've been an incredible doctor, but a pencil pusher he was not. I've been forced to plow through it in chunks while struggling to keep up on current papers. All this administrative crap frustrates me most because it does nothing to directly serve patients.

I KNOW it's pretty unusual for a department head to have a hero complex, but I *have* helped save lives since taking the position. It's just been indirect, not hands-on. But I do everything that I possibly can.

Everything from getting a kid from a poor family a transplant to keeping the department on the cutting edge of modern cardiology medicine; I go after it all with everything I have. I'm not an ex-army tough guy like my Dad, but I still fight—for my patients and for my department. Even if I have to fund the battles with my own money.

THIS MESS with Madelyne is just another day at the office in that respect. I'm trying to save a life. But the question is, how best to do so?

. . .

IF SHE'S SUICIDAL, by law, I'm supposed to turn around and hand her right over to the psychiatric wing for a 48-hour hold. If I don't and she kills herself, I'm liable. But if I do ... she'll end up in the hands of the worst department head on the entire Ravenwood staff.

DR. WESTRIDGE ISN'T JUST a bad doctor, he's a bad administrator. All kinds of rumors fly around this place about the psychiatric wing. Unacceptably high suicide levels. Unexplained deaths. Complaints of abuse.

HE AND I have clashed on a variety of subjects, including his insistence on keeping certain mentally ill cardiac patients in restraints, even when it endangers them. He loves drugs, often keeping his patients on levels of sedatives that sometimes endanger them as well. And he loves petty power plays— even among his equals—making him nearly impossible to work with.

THE REST of us on staff keep hearing reports of complaints and lawsuits filed against Westridge and wonder when he will finally run out of money for settlements. As far as I am concerned, he doesn't belong anywhere near a patient—ever. But so far luck, money, and a talented lawyer have protected him from any serious consequences.

I CAN'T SEND Madelyne to him. I know too well what will happen if I do. The man will make everything worse. He seems to have a talent for it.

. . .

IF I TAKE her across state lines, though, and into a major city like Portland, I can get her into a hospital with someone who has to be more competent and ethical than Westridge. Now that she's starting to calm down, maybe I can get her to agree to that as a plan if she needs to be hospitalized.

WE EMERGE from the access road onto the coastal highway and sweep northward along its cliff-hugging curves, the sea shimmering under the moon to one side of us. I can see the gleam of lights from little hamlets dotting the hills above us, and the sheets of cloud from the dying storm have all lowered into a hilltop crown of fog.

IT'S a view worth living to see. I hope my passenger notices.

I CHECK IN WITH HER, reaching back carefully to pat her hand with my gloved one. She squeezes my fingers briefly and I go back to driving, temporarily satisfied. *Well, she didn't bail back on the road, and I doubt she's going to jump now that we're out here.*

ON WE DRIVE, past several cliffside houses and a rest stop, until finally I slow down to take a break at a turn-off that leads up the hill to my home. It has a couple of benches and an old phone booth. I pull up by one of the benches and get off to stretch my legs and talk to her.

"HOW WAS THAT?" I ask as she awkwardly pulls off her helmet.

. . .

"It was ... a little overwhelming, but I ... I'm glad you took me for a ride. Where are we going?" Her voice sounds so hesitant and tentative that I wonder if she thinks I'm leaving her here.

I open my mouth to offer her a ride back to my place, and then I have to stop and wonder at my motives. *Behave.* "Well," I say slowly, "where do you want to go?"

She looks out over the ocean silently, wrapping her arms around herself. "As far from here as we can," she finally murmurs. "That's where I want to go."

I think about the two days off work I have coming, and mentally count the cash left in my wallet. I live more modestly than I have to, so I usually have a decent amount of liquid assets. I might have to visit a bank at some point, but ...

"Any specifics?" But of course, she shakes her head. She really wasn't thinking past tonight. I'm glad I was smart enough to pick up on that.

"All right, up the coastline it is, then. I'll just get us some clothes to change into in the nearest large town." I give her a smile, and see a gleam of something like hope in her eyes.

If you want to continue reading this story, you can get your copy from your favorite vendor by searching for the title:

Dr. Orgasm
A Virgin and a Billionaire Romance

You can also find the e-book version by typing this link in your computer's browser:

https://www.hotandsteamyromance.com/products/dr-orgasm-a-virgin-and-a-billionaire-romance

OTHER BOOKS BY THIS AUTHOR

Saving Her Rescuer: A Billionaire & A Virgin Romance

I was just trying to get away from my crazy ex for the weekend when I ended up in a giant pileup on the highway up to Gore Mountain.

https://geni.us/SavingHerRescuer

~

Sensual Sounds: A Rockstar Ménage

Lust. Lies. Double lives.

The rock and roll industry is full of people who are looking out for themselves and willing to do anything to rise to the top.

https://www.hotandsteamyromance.com/collections/frontpage/products/sensual-sounds-a-rockstar-menage

~

On the Run: A Secret Baby Romance

Murder. Lies. Fraud. Just another day in the lives of billionaires and women on the run.

https://www.hotandsteamyromance.com/collections/frontpage/products/on-the-run-a-secret-baby-romance

The Dirty Doctor's Touch: A Billionaire Doctor Romance

I am a master. An elitist. I am at the top of my field, and I know what I am doing.

https://www.hotandsteamyromance.com/collections/frontpage/products/the-dirty-doctor-s-touch-a-billionaire-doctor-romance

The Hero She Needs: A Single Daddy Next Door Romance

He's the only man I've ever wanted...

https://www.hotandsteamyromance.com/collections/frontpage/products/the-hero-she-needs-a-single-daddy-next-door-romance

You can find all of my books here

Hot and Steamy Romance

https://www.hotandsteamyromance.com

ABOUT THE AUTHOR

Mrs. Love writes about smart, sexy women and the hot alpha billionaires who love them. She has found her own happily ever after with her dream husband and adorable 6 and 2 year old kids.

Currently, Michelle is hard at work on the next book in the series, and trying to stay off the Internet.

"Thank you for supporting an indie author. Anything you can do, whether it be writing a review, or even simply telling a fellow reader that you enjoyed this. Thanks

 facebook.com/HotAndSteamyRomance
 instagram.com/michellesromance

©Copyright 2020 by Michelle Love - All rights Reserved
In no way is it legal to reproduce, duplicate, or transmit any part of this document in either electronic means or in printed format. Recording of this publication is strictly prohibited and any storage of this document is not allowed unless with written permission from the publisher. All rights are reserved.
Respective authors own all copyrights not held by the publisher.

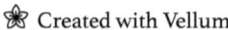 Created with Vellum

www.ingramcontent.com/pod-product-compliance
Lightning Source LLC
LaVergne TN
LVHW021711060526
838200LV00050B/2602